I0707583

silence of my inceptive self

l. smith

Smittyville™—From Standy to Forefront

Dedicated to telling diverse stories that matter and to providing opportunities to move writing projects from standby to the forefront.

more of l. smith

"Black Man Running"
https://newversenews.blogspot.com/2022/02/black-man-running.html

"Does Time Have Color Too?"
https://thenewversenews.substack.com/p/nvn-wednesday-does-time-have-color

"'Worse' Than Rodney King?"
https://newversenews.blogspot.com/2023/01/worse-than-rodney-king.html

www.lsmithwriter.com
x.com/L_Smith_Writer
IG: @l.smith.writer

ISBN: 979-8-218-41117-6
eISBN: 978-0-578-72714-1

Any references to historical events, real people, or real places are used fictitiously. Names, characters, and places are products of the author's imagination.

Front cover image by Smittyville™ LLC.
Book design and inside covers by Smittyville™ LLC.
Author images by Smittyville™ LLC.
Edited by Louise Stahl.
lsmith@lsmithwriter.com

Printed by Smittyville™ LLC, in the United States of America.
First edition, April 2024.

Smittyville™ LLC
5900 Balcones Drive, Ste 100
Austin, Texas 78731
www.smitty-ville.com

for all young women trying to figure it out

"Listen to silence. It has so much to say."

— RUMI

contents

three

four

eight

nine

ten

next

a fore word

S itting on my back porch during the dry season under the cover of Tamarindo trees, one of my best friends, Kimberly, and I wrote our first chapter books. We were 10 years old, living on Clark Air Force Base in the Philippines, and we would meet daily,  painstakingly plotting out the details of each chapter. I titled my book *The World of Cloudious©*, about fictional characters living in the clouds, and I personally typed each chapter, all six of them, on my family's typewriter, whiting-out mistakes as I made them. My book included my hand-drawn illustrations to give a hint to the contents of each chapter. My then stay-at-home mama helped me bind it and create its cover: a blueish gray fabric, representative of the sky in which my characters called home. This unpublished chapter book collecting dust on my bookshelf is of my most valuable possessions—writing that book was likely the first outward expression of the writing gift born in me, the gift that has pursued me throughout my life.

In middle school, a simple haiku of mine was published in a Department of Defense anthology of overseas student writing and artwork. In high school, English classes were my joy. At Texas State University, a college professor reaffirmed my giftedness in writing, and to help decide if a journalism major was what I wanted, I wrote a few articles for the campus newspaper, the *University Star*. I was good at journalistic writing but subconsciously realized it didn't match the fulfillment I received from completing that chapter book years earlier. Thus, my degree path shifted, and I left Texas State University with a degree in mass communications, an advertising focus, and retaining writing aspirations, I minored in writing. To fulfill writing minor credits, I began creative writing again, completing poems and prose, which made for great therapy in processing my daddy's passing of colon cancer, breakups, unrequited love, and other twenty-something- year-old experiences.

Upon graduating from Texas State, a media planning position opened at a local ad agency where I interned, and I landed my first professional job, as a media planner for the southwest markets of a large mobile service provider, researching cellular phone user demographics, competitor's advertising strategies and market share, later adding media buyer for the northeast markets of a major retailer to my title and responsibilities. This agency scored big with a subsequent large pitch and, in turn, multiplied its staff and office space. I hired my own assistant and managed several interns. I busted out media plans, doubling my income in less than a year, having received praise from supervisors, but my biggest score was a large dose of burn-out, questioning the relevance of TV and radio spots airing, newspaper ads running. I was writing, *a lot*, including contributing articles for the company newsletter, but that type of writing wasn't bringing fulfillment equal to that first chapter book I wrote in the Philippines.

Desiring to find more meaningful work, I resigned, picked up journalism again (peppering it over providing customer service for a major apparel retailer, selling computers for a major computer retailer, and ghost-writing columns for the executive director of a non-profit), freelancing for *The Pflugerville Pflag* and *The Villager*, and had a baby girl. I covered stories about Houston residents taking refuge in Austin after hurricane Rita, the expansion of the Austin Community College, and lighter stories like decluttering homes for spring cleaning. There was a satisfaction in seeing and reading my writing in print, but the routine of writing news stories again felt hollow.

My daughter, a toddler, and my marriage, rocked by financial strain, I needed more than freelance and call-center income. A lengthy job-search finally produced a writing position at an elections company with clients in counties in Texas, Hawaii, Colorado, Tennessee, and Illinois. The training director, a former teacher, interviewed me, zoned in on the instructor in me, and informed that the writing position was filled, but he needed trainers. I accepted, working the next year as a traveling technical trainer, teaching county staff and poll workers to operate the company's voting system, designed to fulfill the requirements of the Help America Vote Act (HAVA). I traveled the majestic mountains of Colorado, the quaint and isolated counties of Texas, the islands of Hawaii, the green-expanse of Tennessee, and the cold busyness of Chicago, helping to make counties HAVA-compliant, neglecting freelance news writing, and largely, my own creative writing, and missing my daughter. When the HAVA mission was accomplished, the company downsized, and thank God that the downsizing included me, as traveling and missing my toddler was taxing, and that the instructor in me had been excavated.

The training director, even though he left the profession because the salary was inadequate to support his family of five, suggested that I give teaching a try during our brief, surreal downsizing meeting. I explored his advisement by substitute teaching.

Soon, I entered an accelerated teaching certification program, Texas Teaching Fellows, through which I obtained special education and English teaching certificates, followed by master reading teacher, and later, several more teaching certificates while working for the University of Texas Charter School system, including English as a Second Language and two secondary history certificates. My teaching career birthed a campus newsletter, co-teaching a writing program with an Austin Community College professor, Irwin Tang, and inspiration for my students to unleash their pain with the pen. I compiled their powerful, poignant hurts, plus fiction, into two anthologies, first, *Voices*© and next, *Sunrays and Shadows*©, letting the process of designing our anthologies inspire me to revisit my own writing—enough for my own book.

This collection of writing, compiled over 20 years, but mostly written as a 20-something year old with topics that span dating, flirting, heartbreak, death of my daddy, marital bliss and frustration, all from a relatable but youthful perspective, along with reflections of my daughter in toddlerhood from me as a first-time mom, some erotica (yes, moms are still sexual beings), short stories, life reflective prose, and reflections of God in prose, and talks that I gave in-person to the women's ministry and full-on congregation at my church, reflect a journey through life and maturation, through living for the world to living for higher purpose, through confusion to enlightenment.

This collection of writing, though real and raw, but also, hopefully, playful, and light-hearted, is also stamped with God's footprints, with His loving kindness, grace, and mercy having chased me down and covered me all throughout my life and with Him having carried me through events in my life, especially those dark moments. I am grateful to God giving me the courage to just do it— just put my writing "out there," assuring me that I'm not the first and won't be the last to emote the way my words reflect on these pages, and reassuring me that He's gifted me uniquely to share these works with you. I am grateful to God for giving me the gift of written communication, be it creative or otherwise. And, I am grateful for all my supporters, and inspiration, you know who you are and have been over the years, but I'll call out my supportive mother, Linda, and a most surprising support source of late, my daughter, who, since she was born has never ceased to amaze me with the wisdom that God's instilled in her. To paraphrase Rumi, I let the strange pull of what I really love draw me into this collection of writing. I hope you do too. ☺ And, I hope this collection of writing makes you feel something.

silence of my inceptive self

collected writings, volume one

one

"If you become silent after your laughter, one day you will hear
God also laughing, you will hear the whole existence laughing —
trees and stones and stars with you."

— OSHO

silence of whimsy

life's punchline revealed,
bluff called, words winking at life—
a mocking. Selah.

silence of my inceptive self

finally
I am alone
sitting here all alone
no phone ringing, just silence
no one boring me with the details
of their uneventful day
no children to entertain
no friends to complain
no phone ringing – just silence
sitting here all alone
enjoying myself,
thinking of me and
being me and
just acting selfishly
and thinking of what I want to be
happening
next in my life
and suddenly
it dawns on me
that right now
more than anything
the one thing
I want to be
happening
more than anything
else
is to be
listening
to the phone ring
just to break the
silence of my
self.

(and my own uneventful day).

the shirt

I took the shirt that
I bought for you
from your closet and
wore it.
I did not ask
you if I could. I just did.
You were probably saving
it for some
special occasion. It was so
pretty. I could
not resist. I
should not have given
it
to you.
I apologize for spilling
grape juice
on it this morning.
It still had the
tag
on it.

creative process

I have these thoughts and
I write them down
and them come back to
them after better words
are found and
then I switch them around
and say them out loud to
see how they sound.
see if there's a pattern
or a rhythm.
then I share them with my
husband to see if
they make sense to him
or if he can relate
of if there's something
about them that he
might hate. and if so,
then I think it must
be a go because if he
can feel that strongly
about them, then I must
have written something
right something,
real. after all,
I did make him
feel.

watermelon

green oval
swollen pink
seedy,
juicy,
refreshing,
just like you.

doctor's visit

So many people
Just like me? No they can't be,
It must be something worse.
I try to see clues to their woes,
looking them up and down,
but, I still don't get it.
I stare at their faces to get at their agony,
but, I have no clue. They compose too well.
They're reading the newspaper
just like me, only they ain't.
I choose to write—to
write what I see.
To pass the time? Or
to hush the whine the
whine of constant pain, maybe not
pain. Pressure, frustration, irritation?
Maybe nothing at all. No it can't be. But
there's no pain for me. No pressure, frustration, irritation
but I have reason. A concern. And
I'm gonna see.
I'm gonna see what it's all about.
Doc might think it's silly.
He might think it's just me,
But still I'm gonna see.
Maybe there's not that many people. But people just the same.
You think they're wondering back about me?
Because I'll sure enough tell them. Tell them good and to the
point.
Are they just like me? No they can't be.
It must be something worse.

graduation

Red caps and gowns tall and short,
fat and thin, gathered in the foyer
from A to Z for the procession.
Cameras flashed at the graduates lined side by side
with their arms around each other's shoulders,
smiling proudly, crossed eyes, rabbit ears,
scrunched noses, stuck out tongues....
The black gown gave the final call.
The uninflated beach ball was folded and tucked into the red
gown.
The bubble-blowing kit stashed in a shirt pocket.
The gowns straightened the line, straightened their caps and fixed
their ties.
Shaky legs, sweaty palms and teary eyes marched one by one
through the double doors some too quickly, others too slow,
some with a sassy strut, others with a timid pace.
Each ear passed the through the double doors
immediately filled with pomp and circumstance,
and every face began to beam.
Their eyes began searching for mom, dad, and grandma,
but were blinded by the lights and their own frantic excitement.
One of them could hear her little brother
screaming her name hysterically above the rest of the audience.
Her eyes rolled; cheeks turned red
as she envisioned all eyes of the audience fixed on her blushed
face.
The senile great aunt halted the entire procession to
snap her graduate who was the first A of the line.
He yelled his aunt's name in astonishment,
his blushed face flashed a wide smile,
then he quickly led her to the rest of the family.

Row by row was filled by the red gowns as they stood
and waited for every seat to filled and then they all sat as one body.
The N in the middle row began to wail uncontrollably
and the M right next to her whipped out his beach ball
and busied himself filling it with air to keep himself from wailing
also.
The whole red-capped class filled
like the beach ball
with anxiety
and anticipation of what's next.

full of yourself

why you think
all my poems
are about you?
that they all
have to be true?
I am an artist,
a wordsmith
with imagination
like butter.
I got skills.
I take teeny tiny
elements of reality
and spin them into
make believe.
think just a little bit
more of me.
think that I have
creativity.
my poems are
about me
and my
ingenuity.
you need to
get over yourself.

blank page

Blank page
Has the potential to be great
But instead you're blank
Staring back at me
Bright white
Rectangle
A reflection
Of thoughts
Uncollected

audacity

The doorbell rang, and I went to answer the door knowing that Sarah had finally arrived to my high school graduation celebration. Monica, Kara, and I had been anxiously awaiting Sarah's arrival because we didn't know how to get to the graduation party and were going to follow her.

"Who is it?" my mom asked.

"It's Sarah."

"Well, tell her to c'mon in—there's plenty of food."

Sarah came in, and I shut the door, leading her to the dining room where Monica, Kara, and the rest of my graduation party attendees were.

"Where's Layla? I asked Sarah as we walked down the hallway.

"That girl is outside in the car drunk!" Sarah snickered.

My walking halted.

"Are you serious!" I was livid—I could not believe that Layla would come to my house drunk knowing that everyone's parents were there. I was terrified that, if my parents and Monica and Kara's parents found out that Layla was drunk, they would not let us go to what was going to be the BEST graduation party ever! I was fearful of what they would all think of Layla because our parents didn't know her that well—had never met her, just knew that she was sometimes my ride to and from work on the second shift.

I made a bee line for the front door, hoping to discreetly go outside to check on Layla. Sarah followed me outside.

Walking down the sidewalk, I heard my front door close; Monica and Kara, realizing that Sarah and I were outside, came out as well.

"Crap!" I thought to myself. "So much for discretion."

A line of three 18-year-olds and one 17-year-old marched inquisitively and frustratedly out to a Ford Taurus that was Sarah's car. Through the car's window, I could see that a drunken Layla was laughing and babbling to herself and struggling to get out of the back seat of the car, which I knew we could not let happen. Monica and Kara stood beside Sarah and me in front of the car door peering with amazement at Layla—we'd never been drunk before.

Realizing the weight of this situation, my amazement quickly turned to indignation. I was thinking I may as well kiss living on campus at college goodbye. Annoyed and nervous, I didn't want to make a scene and let on to my parents, to *all* the parents, that something was going down outside.

In desperation, I turned to Monica and Kara.

"Layla's drunk in there!" I told them, in captain obvious fashion, and then I noticed Monica's younger sister, Freesia, walking over to Sarah's car; she must have realized that all of us were missing and made the decision to do some recon.

My temples began to pulse. I waved my hand in the air motioning Freesia to go back inside my house. Surely, she would see Layla and tell the parents everything! Freesia did not turn back but quickened her pace while smiling at me. And behind her, I saw my mom. My eyes grew wide. My mom was walking over in our direction—she must have seen Freesia leave the house and realized that all the graduates, my friends and I, were all outside gathered at Sarah's car. Not sure what to do, I looked at a drunk Layla, then looked back at the house to see yet another mom walking over to Sarah's car—Kara's mom was on her way over, too.

I could not believe that this was happening, and my annoyance grew to infuriation with Kara and Monica because they drew the matter to everyone's attention when they followed us outside. Lucky for us, rather than approaching Sarah's car, the mom's stopped at the end of the sidewalk.

"What's going on?" my mom asked.

"Nothing!" I snapped, "We just wanted to see Sarah's new car!"

"Hi, Mrs. Stevens!" yelled drunken Layla to my mom through a rear Taurus window that she'd managed to partially roll down, and I thought perhaps I should find a shovel and start digging our graves because I just knew we all were going to be dead.

"Oh, snap!" said Freesia.

"Shut it!" Monica yelled at her sister, as she grabbed her by the elbow and pulled her close.

The tense torsos of Monica, Kara, Sarah, and I were an unlikely but fortunate and impenetrable fortress blocking Sarah's Taurus' windows from the moms' line of sight, so they couldn't see Layla wrestling with the door lock and with herself to get up out the back seat of the sedan.

"Hi, Layla!" my mom shouted back, as she started to approach the car. Motivated by my mom's voice, Layla tried a bit harder to unlock the rear Taurus door, and with lucky success, she quickly swung one short, inebriated leg out the door.

Sarah quickly shoved Layla and her drill team leg back in the back seat, shut the door, and walked to the car's driver's side hoping to indicate to the moms that she was about to leave. She was embarrassed, too, and thought that this gesture would keep the posse of moms from further approaching the car. The rest of us quickly turned around and started walking coolly back to the house, blocking the sidewalk path that the moms were taking to the car. We and the moms met face to face, and I told my mom that Sarah and Layla were waiting for us to get our purses so we could go to the party. The moms hesitated a moment. They looked at each other as if to say "OK" and turned around, leading us all back into the house.

We were spared from mom wrath, better yet, *dad* wrath, because they were indoors, at my graduation party as well.

I was relieved that the audacity drove away in the Taurus.

music

music is my inspiration
motivation
daily meditation
my private ovation
my invitation to get moving

imagination

My imagination
has an imagination of its own.
You can't tell me you have something
          important to tell me
And then leave me
                              hanging
What if
          you have cancer and you only have 6 weeks to live?
What if
          she got into a car wreck and is in the hospital clinging to
life?
What if
          you saw him cheating with my best girlfriend?
Just *tell me.*
          The same effort
          it took you to tell me you have *something*
          important
To tell me could have been used to just
          tell it.
Otherwise, I'll create something much worse,
          because my imagination has an imagination of its own.

my spoken word

you think I'm crazy
sending you all my poetry?
well it's my way of sharing me
with you of getting you to
see me, know me on
the inside and all
of my complexities
my sexuality,
spirituality,
intellectuality,
insecurities,
my feelings
because often
I can't express them
verbally.
you feel me?
my poetry
is my spoken
word.

two

"To be intimate is to feel the silence, the space that everything is happening in."

— ADYASHANTI

silence of my loins

who would have thought that
deep within the sultry flesh
lies another pulse.

burn

My heartbeat
burns a constant bonfire.
You set it
ablaze long before we
even said hello.
Just the sight of you
was enough
to light the spark.
I lay awake at night
wondering if you
lay awake too.

if

if only you knew
what I think when
I think about you,
you wouldn't think
I'm as shy as I seem.
if only you knew
what I think when
I think about you,
you would believe
what I say when
I say what I mean.
if only you knew
what I think when
I think about you,
you would be thinking
of me all day too.
if only you knew
what I think when
I think about you,
you'd want me to
do what I do and
keep doing it to you.
if only you knew
what I think when
I think about you,
you wouldn't think
I'm as sweet as
you believe.
if only you knew
what I think when
I think about you,

you wouldn't think
I'm just a tease.
if you only knew
what I felt when
I think about you,
then you'd want
to feel me too.
if you only knew
what I touch when
I think about you,
then you'd want
to touch it too.
if you only knew
what I do when
I think about you,
then you'd want to
join in…

can't stop

Heart flutters
Smiles all day
Stomach jitters
Silly girly
Tears
Dreams
Shatters
What-ifs
Can't bees
Why me
Can't sleep
Can't stop
You
Every minute
You
Are there

incubation

tonight
I'm writing poetry
about you.
don't even know what to say,
can't describe how you make me feel.
ever love someone before you know them—that
love that's like childbirth that's
growing, moving, expanding,
bursting, wonderful, amazing?

processing

God, I pray it's from you.
These feelings, I pray they're from you.
They're too dangerous to not be.
Lord, I pray you have something
wonderful in store for me—something
I've not imagined before,
something I can't even fathom.
I pray.

who?

told my mama 'bout you.
I don't even know you.
told my best friend 'bout you.
who are you?
who I am? they say.
they don't know me.
I don't know you.
we'll see.

spinning

running across my heart
I feel you
Inside my chest
In the dark.
I still see you.
God help me
stop spinning.
I need both feet on the ground.
I don't know you,
only said two words to you.
Lord help me
stop spinning.
Lord, let it be real.
when it stops spinning,
what's it going to feel
like?
please let it be real.
I do want to feel
again.
love
again.
trust
again.

you

you inspire me
Ignite me
Exhaust me
Drain me
Shame me
Lift me
Shame me
Lift me
Embarrass me
Belittle me
Lift me
Lift me
Lift me
Make me
see me with you.

penetration

can you get inside
split it open wide
not between my thighs
inside my mind
crack it open wide
massage it slow
make it go
make it flow
fast with thoughts
I never thought before
realization
imagination
stimulation
penetration
not vaginally
but mentally
that's what you got to give me
penetration of the cranium
come over here and give me some
I am open wide
just waiting for you to come inside
make me see the light
the moon the stars the sun
make me believe you are the one
I can take it
Give me all you got
give it to me hard and raw and deep
make it so good I cannot speak
tell me your dreams your fears your goals
tell me those things no one knows
tell me about your history

and then what you plan to be
twenty, thirty years from now
and then tell me your plan of how
you intend to do it
do it
do it good
damn, baby I knew you could
just look past my womanhood
my sexuality
because there's so much more to me
than that.
so keep your jimmy hat
in your pocket
rip the phone cord from the socket
turn the lights down low
hell, turn them out and lock the door
because all I need is your mouth
and your lips and your tongue
I don't care about how well you're hung
just give me your mouth
and lick my mind
til it's soak and wet
make me squirm and make me sweat
complete saturation
penetration
of the cranium
I'm diggin your rhythm
colloquialism
the words you choose
and how you put them together
you got me floatin like a feather
just lick your lips and tell me more….
penetrate me to the core
and I'll keep receiving you

til I can't take it no more
say it brotha
do it daddy
and I'll ride with you like you're my caddie
take me where I need to go
elevate me to a new plateau
enter my mind and just beat it
beat it like a drum
beat it til the battle's won
do it and do it and do it wild
do it like it's going out of style
smack it up, flip it, rub it down
shake it all the way to the ground
or just sit in it
and stroke it slow
make it melt like a pot of gold
swing it to the left side and then the right
just put it down all through the night
or just marinate it or
let it simmer
keep on til I get the shivers
keep on til it swells and blisters
ooh wee
I want it so badly
school me learn me educate me
stimulate me
penetrate me
intellectually
this is my fantasy
this is my wet dream
I long for it
I live for it
why
do you make me beg for it?

won't you give it to me daddy?
please?
don't you see?
then, that penetration you need
will come
so naturally
will come
so
deep
but only
if we were meant to be
so let us first connect
mentally
and see.
shall we?

soften

you soften me
habitually
in you I dissolve like
sugar refined
in water as one
we become
sweetened, sticky
tasty with flavor changing
like the seasons fall
and spring mild
with texture soft
as wet ashes deliberate
and thick like
molasses slow
like wine together
we age with distinguished
savor soft
on the pallet
gently touched
by a love
memorable.

last night

Last night I listened to you breathe
and your exhale entered me
like slow smoke fills a room.
last night I felt your heart beat
inside the palm of my hand
and felt its rhythm quicken
with each strike of the nearing thunder.
you turned me inside and out and outside and in
you twisted me and rearranged me
like I was your rubix cube and
you wanted to make all my colors
match up
you had me going down like a slinky
unable to walk straight think straight
you had me like a game of Scrabble
with letters every where
and I was unable to form the right words
to tell you just how you made
me feel….
you had me feeling so out of character,
out of place
like
I was your left shoe on your right foot…
you kneaded me and rolled me and flattened me right out
like you were my baker and I your dough
and then you got me nice and hot
and watched me rise up all over again….

spring fever

I have the fever
for the flavor
of you
spring is here
I am too
so what are
you going to do?

spring is here
and I'm in bloom
catch my tune?
come pick my flower
you got me feeling like
an april shower
wet and warmth
covering me
like a yellow swarm
of honey bees
fluttering closely
trying to taste my
sweet nectar.
I'm feeling pink
like the peonies
amidst the bluebonnets
I'd like to sit down and
write me a sonnet
about you but I
got the fever or
rather, the fever
got me
warm and sticky

I need something cool
I need a pool
a splash of you
I need a sparkling
drink of you.
spring is here
I am too
so what are you
going to do?
come blow on me
with a flurry so I
can float like
the dandelions
light and airy
and drift past
the dragonflies
as far as the wind
can carry
then I'd land
on your knee
delicately
like a lady bug
like your little
lady, but I won't be
buggin and you'll know
it's me and you won't be
shruggin me away as I make
my way up your thigh
savoring the flavor
of you.
spring is here and
I have arrived
let me share with you
my high

I'm feeling very green
not like envy
but like the toad
you know that
toad, that
horny one
let's go sit in
the grass and set
like the sun
and have some
fun watering my
flower so we both
can feel like
april showers
hear that tune?
spring is here
and I'm in bloom and
that fever just won't
release me. and
your flavor, honey?
just like blackberry
stains me
eternally
(or at least just
enough to make
it through next
winter's melting snow).

charade

I know you're admiring me.
You think because you don't look me in the eye that I don't know?
I can feel your eyes piercing my back.
You think because you don't say "hi" that I'll think otherwise?
I know you're telling your friends about me.
I saw them all look over here.
You think because you don't turn around
when I walk by that I'll think you don't care?
My girlfriend saw you look me up and down
from head to breast to legs to feet.
You really think I don't know?
Think you can shoo your craving away?
With me, it don't work that way—
you can eat everything under the sun,
but your heart will still growl until you
devour that which you crave.
How long do you think you can pretend?
I know you want me,
But you know you can't handle this, though.

poorly written

When I first saw you,
I knew who you were.
You were meant for me.
Before we even spoke,
I knew who you were.
Before I even knew your name,
before you even said hello,
I knew who you were.
You were meant for me.
I have no words to describe
what I felt when I first saw you,
but what I know is that
you are meant for me.

play

can you come out and play?
let's fly your kite
swim in your pool
swing on your swings
climb in your tree
i can't wait to play with you
let me share your jellybeans
I'll give you some ice cream
or maybe a blowpop
let me ride your bike
join your secret club
read your book
go in your treehouse
i can't wait to play with you
let me share your crayons
to draw a picture of you and me
I'll give you some jax
or maybe some pick-up
sticks
let me slide down your slide
make me go up high
on the see-saw
let's go round and round
til we're dizzy on the merry-go-round
let me hold your action figure
i can't wait to play with you
let me borrow your boomerang
and I'll give you some pie,
it's lemon meringue
let me throw your frisbee
and you can through it back

to me
let me hula-hoop with you
shoot your marbles
I'll go hide and if you
promise to come and seek
i can't wait to play with you
you can be the doctor
and I'll be real sick
and if I misbehave you
can tap me with the yardstick
you can be the teacher
and I'll be your student
you can grade my paper
and tell me how well I did.
Wanna play?

every possible way

I miss you beside me
behind me
beneath me
on top of me.
And my lips miss your tongue.
My fingers miss your fingers.
My waist misses your arm.
My breasts miss your hands.
My nipples miss your tongue.
My neck misses your lips.
My body misses your weight.
My navel misses your tongue.
My eyes miss your face.
My skin misses your skin.
My legs miss your back.
My ass misses your hands.
My chest misses your head.
My skin misses your sweat.
My ears miss your moans.
My back misses your palms.
My cheek misses your breath.
My hips miss your hips.
My ass misses your hips
My mouth misses the insides
of your thighs.
My hands miss your buttocks.
My tongue misses your nipples.
My lips miss your navel.
I want you beside me
on top of me
beneath me
behind me.
I want you in every way possible.

preoccupied

you are so preoccupied
you don't even notice me
and so, I'm never satisfied
but that's what keeps me mystified
the fact that I can't get enough of you
because you don't have enough of
you to give. you specified
that you needed to be preoccupied
emotionally, because you are terrified
to let love find you and that's sad
because it makes you desensitized. you
are afraid to feel. dehumanized. denying
that which makes you human. unless
all that was just a lie
to keep me hypnotized
and to make me want to try
to get you to love me
but I can't ever tell you
not that I'm shy, it's just
that you keep me tongue-tied
touching on my thighs
and on that you capitalize
why can't you open your eyes?
and look through your heart
I promise you, you'll be surprised
because I've loved you from the start
you're just so damn preoccupied
touching on my thighs
you will probably never notice

cute day

Every time the phone rang, Anne's heart raced. She swung quickly around in her ergonomic swivel chair to stare at the lips of the person who answered the phone. She was trying to read them before they hollered the name of the person the caller was asking for.

"Stephanie! Telephone!"

Stephanie will be on the phone for the next half hour. If someone tries to get through, they'll get a busy signal because this business phone, as illogical as this sounds, doesn't have call waiting or voice mail.

Anne slowly swung her chair away from the person at the phone. She made a couple of complete circles with her eyes closed and head tilted completely back, preparing herself to square off with the little green screen again. The phone, just a few feet away, was her escape from the green screen. Unfortunately, it was everyone's escape. She worked with at least fifteen others in her area. Many of her coworkers had children, many of them had wives, many of them had husbands and most of the time, many of these people called. So, the phone, supposedly for emergency calls only, rang constantly—that is, when it wasn't constantly in use. Little did they know; this *was* an emergency. It was an emergency that she talks to Eric. For tonight, he was Anne's escape.

"Stupid motherfucker!" Stephanie grunted as she slammed the phone down. Everyone knows Stephanie is married so she has her boyfriend call her at work. He calls her every hour on the hour. Seven out of eight calls are heated ones, and Stephanie doesn't care who knows or overhears. All is forgotten when she picks up that phone. Every conversation she has ends with eyes rolling, lips smacking, an "asshole" or if she's really irate, a "motherfucker", like tonight, and a slam of the receiver. This time, all of that took three minutes flat. This is definitely a record for Stephanie. As soon as the receiver touched the base, the phone rang short double rings again. This meant an outside call.

"Anne! Telephone!"

Anne hoped that this was the call she'd been waiting all night for. She had been sitting at this machine for eight hours straight—put a panel on the table, hit the buttons, take a panel off the table, put a panel on, the buttons, take it off, etc.—praying that the end of this interminable night at work would come. With less than an hour to go, she was beginning to think that she wouldn't hear from him.

Anne swung from the box screen and leaped from her highchair all in one movement. One of her three-inch heels slipped on the newly waxed floor as she dashed through the analyze and repair station to get to the phone.

Three-inch heels and a manufacturing plant don't mix well, but every Friday night is a *cute day*. Almost a year ago, Stephanie and Anne went through orientation together. Since then, Anne has gone to Stephanie's wedding, gotten to know Stephanie's husband and two children, and although she hasn't met him, Stephanie has come to know everything there is to know about Anne's boyfriend. They take lunches and breaks together and pick each other up for work and drop each other at home when necessary.

And, to amuse themselves in this monotonous job, they declared every Friday is a cute day in which Anne and Stephanie adorn themselves in makeup, jewelry, heels, the works, get their hair done and sometimes even wear dresses to work where they are surrounded by forklifts, pallets, smocks, gloves and safety glasses. The additional unspoken reason for Stephanie being that she's trying to pick up another boyfriend. The additional reason for Anne being that she never knows exactly what she will do Friday night after work. Sometimes a girlfriend will call wanting to go to a club, or a guy friend wanting to go to a movie, or Eric wanting her to come over. Sometimes she'll just go home. But she never knows, so she goes to work on Friday nights in "going-out" clothes, because she lives too far from work and everything else to change at home after work. By the time she drives home, changes clothes, and drives to wherever she is going to go, it's one o'clock in the morning, if not later, and most things in this town shut down at two.

"Whuzzup?" Eric's voice penetrated the receiver, and its thickness seeped into Anne's ear and spread all throughout her body. The end of the unyielding night at work has come.

"Nothin'. Whatcha doin'?"

"Listening to music and thinking about you."

"Oh, yeah?"

"Uh-huh. Whatcha doin tonight?"

"Well, that depends on you. What*choo* doin tonight?"

"I wanna see you."

"Oh yeah? Where do you wanna go?"

"Nowhere. I want you to come over here."

"Where's Cynthia?"

"She went to Hutto for the weekend."

"What's in Hutto?"

"Her sister."

"Oh. Is your son home?"

"Naw. She took him, too."

"So, you are really chilllin' tonight, huh?"

"Yeah. So whuzzup?"

"It'll take me about 20 minutes to get over there because I have to get some gas and something to sip on."

"Do you remember how ta get over here?"

"Yeah, I remember. Which car did she take?"

"She took the 'Lac. So, the green one is in the drive. Park on the side of the house, though, all right? I have some nosy neighbors, man."

"All right then. See ya in a few."

Anne gently placed the phone on the hook. She was trying to calm the delight she felt stirring in her body so that she wouldn't be so obvious to her coworkers. She felt as though they had heard her conversation and could read the thoughts brewing in her mind. Anne could not stifle the delight, and it wormed out from between her lips and formed a smile as she walked back to the machine, careful this time, so that she wouldn't slip on those heels.

She was thrilled that she had finally made some plans for tonight. She didn't know what she was going to do if Eric hadn't called. Felicia had a date with Robert—she told Anne his name, like Anne was supposed to know who he was. Every week it's somebody new for Felicia. Renada never goes out. A Friday night for her is renting the '70-something "Black Shampoo" which she's already seen four times and watching it while eating chocolate-covered strawberries. Sue and Kimika rededicated their lives to God a while back and so they stopped going out. Jamaal was out of town, but that was good because Anne didn't wanna see his boring ass anyway. All he ever talked about was going to Atlanta. Anne wished he'd get his fat ass up and carry it on down there. She hadn't memorized Trey's number yet and forgot to bring it to work so she couldn't call him. She refused to call Sean until he called her first. Last time they talked, he hung up in her face, angry because she will not and cannot commit to him. So, Eric was Anne's last hope for tonight.

Anne had already told Aaron that she was going to a frat party with Felicia so that in case he calls to check on her, she'd have an alibi. In addition to that, today is a *cute day*. Anne couldn't let a *cute day* and an alibi go to waste. It had been almost a month since

Anne had been out or even had a drink because of all the overtime she had been working and the heap of essays essays she's had to write for her courses. This was long overdue.

Anne pounced back into the highchair and glared into the green screen. Every night was a battle with that machine to see who or what would give in first. Either the machine would break down or Anne would fall asleep. Tonight, was more like a draw. The machine didn't break down, and Anne didn't drift off. But she still felt like she had won because the little screen hadn't swallowed her up in its deep, green boredom. Now that Anne had some plans, the last forty-five minutes flew by. "Fuck you," Anne said to the machine as she turned it off. She walked out of the blue double doors.

✱ ✱

Anne got into her little black '83 Toyota Tercel. Actually, it's two-toned; it's white on the roof where the paint has been worn off. The night was clear but very cold. Anne dreaded the cold because her heater only worked when she's driving 55 mph or above. She was always the last to drive out of the plant parking lot because it takes the car at least ten minutes to warm up. She sat there on the cold leather impatiently waiting for it to warm and thinking about Eric while her coworkers honked and zipped by—Stephanie, Sarah, John in their Sonata, Supra and Land Cruiser. Eric was probably lying butt naked on the couch with his dick in his hand, watching a flick as he always does when he is home alone. The engine was warm now.

Anne put the clutch down and drove out of the empty lot. She pulled into the Exxon right across the street which was convenient because the bitch-light (the light on the dash shaped like a gas tank that seems to say, "Bitch, you need some gas!") was glowing red. She got five dollars on number five, a Break the Bank scratch-off, a Styrofoam cup with ice, straw, and a bottle of Wild Apple Boones.

Once back inside the Tercel, all Anne wanted to do was get on the highway so that she could go fifty-five to thaw out her numb fingers, toes and ears lobes.

She clicked on the radio. It resembled a pull-out but was more like a "dangle-out" because it dangled out of the hole in which was supposed to be seated. She poured the Boones in the cup, took a sip and she started for the highway.

If she could remember where Eric lived, it would take her another fifteen or twenty minutes to get there. The last and only other time Anne visited Eric's house was three months ago. He called her early one morning, right after Cynthia went to work. Anne felt like a fool getting up at 7:30 in the morning and driving across town just to get her groove on. So, there they were, that morning in Eric's son's bed (they used Eric Jr's bed out of respect for Cynthia) fucking. Eric Jr. was home that morning. Eric set him up in front of the VCR with the Lion King video to keep him busy. But being the curious three-year-old that he was, Eric Jr. kept getting up to see what "Daddy and that lady" were doing in the room. Anne even though Eric Jr. saw her naked when he forced his big head through the cracked door. Eric kept the door cracked so he could keep an ear on Eric Jr. Good thing for Eric that his son has a limited vocabulary. Thinking about it now, Anne cannot believe that she did that.

Anne touched the metal stub where the volume knob used to exist to turn up the radio. At the light, she turned right. It won't be long now before the heater kicks in. She took a long drag from the straw. The Boones was smooth and sparkling as it slid down her throat. It was also helping to thaw out her insides.

But she needed it desperately. It had been eight endless months since Anne had been kissed, caressed, touched. Eight months ago, her boyfriend was sent to Germany to do a one-year tour. Just four more months and Anne would have made it unkissed, uncaressed and untouched until Aaron returned. But Eric had broken her will.

She took three more long drags from the straw. The R&B radio channel was slowing the music down. As "Emotions" by H-Town streamed from the speakers, her body gave in to the alcohol and the song flooded Anne's mind with memories of her and Eric.

They used to work together at the computer company that Eric still works at. He caught Anne's eye the first time she saw him. He towered six feet four-inch fine frame, draped with bright, monotoned mahogany skin that bowed, twined and rippled over expansive shoulders, a washboard stomach, and solidly rounded thick buttocks and thighs. Eric had an angular jaw structure etched with a goatee, an inviting wide mouth with smooth thin pink lips, two beautiful large nostrils adorned with cat-eyeglasses, cinnamon eyes, broad palms, long fingers and most importantly, big feet. But Anne couldn't let him know that she had noticed him. But hell—with his height, no one could miss him.

❀ ❀

One day at work, Anne was in the crowded breakroom trying to find some where to sit. Eric was already seated with a couple of coworkers. He saw Anne trying hard to find a seat and he blurted out, "I got a seat for you right here."

Anne heard his voice and looked around to see exactly who Eric was talking to. Eric was pointing at the empty chair directly across from his own. Then she realized that he was talking to her. She paused. She could not believe that he had spoken to her. She could not believe that he had even noticed her. Coolly, Anne walked over to his table and sat down.

"What's your name?" Eric said.

"Anne Johnson."

"Do you have a man, Anne Johnson?"

"Is that the way you approach people? I don't even know your name."

"Eric. Well, I just wanna know. Do you?"

"Yes, I do."

"Do you live with him?"

"No. I live with my parents."

"Are you married?"

"No."

"Good. Neither am I. You know somethin?"

"No. What?"

"You have some big, sexy-ass lips. How old are you?"

"I'm twenty-one." There were a million and one things Anne could have said to compliment Eric's looks but she chose to keep them to herself. She was sure that he knew damn well just how good he looked especially because of the way he carried himself. So, Anne simply said, "How old are you?"

"Twenty-five."

"I see. Look—do you have a woman?"

"Naw."

The coworkers that were seated around Eric started to laugh. They could not believe that Eric had just lied to Anne. Well, actually they could. But it was funny anyhow.

"Yes, you do, man," Dwan fessed up for Eric.

"I was bullshittin'. Yeah, I got a woman. I live with her, too. I got a son, too."

Anne was sitting there at the table unable to believe what she was hearing. She could not believe that this man with his woman and his child was trying to talk to her. And then he tried to lie to her about his family. She wondered if Eric would have told her the truth if his coworkers had not fessed up.

"You got a lot of nerve," Anne said. "I really didn't wanna know if you had a woman. I just wanted to let you hear how you sound."

"Well, now that you know, can I have your number?"

"Doesn't it bother you that I have a man?"

"Nope. If you didn't have a man, I wouldn't have asked you for your number."

"And why is that?"

"Because if you didn't have one, then you would be wanting to spend all of your time with me, and I can't do that because I have a woman. It's better this way."

"Oh yeah?"

"Yeah. So, can I have it?"

"I don't think my man would like that. And I know your woman won't like that. I'm not even sure if I would like that."

Anne had two minutes to get back to her workstation. On that note, she stood up.

"I'll see you around Eric."

"Yeah, I know you will."

"Smart ass," Anne said under her breath as she walked back to her area smiling from ear to ear. She was angry that Eric had the audacity to approach her regardless of his girlfriend. But at the very same time Anne was fascinated that this good-looking man, that she had noticed from day one, had noticed her too.

For the next two days, Anne and Eric sat together during breaks and lunch dragging out the same conversation they had the first time they met. And every day Eric asked Anne for her phone number. Each time Anne declined to give it until the fourth day. Finally, Eric said that if she didn't give her number to him this time, he would never ask her again. Anne was seriously considering giving him her phone number, and she was shocked at her own audacity. But Eric was so good looking. Besides, at this point she had been with Aaron for seven months. She was only twenty-one. She was too young to be committed to one man. Ultimately, Anne gave in.

❋ ❋

Anne took another drag from the straw. Her cup was empty now. She reached for the bottle of Boones from the passenger seat. She was so lost in thought that she hadn't realized that her little Tercel was singeing with heat now. She realized that the Boones probably had a lot to do with it, but she cracked the car window any way. Anne also lost track of how fast she was going until she saw blue and red lights dancing in her rear-view mirror. She looked at the speedometer. She had been driving 80 mph on the 55mph highway. She pressed on the brakes hard.

"Shit!" Anne said aloud.

She wondered how long she had been driving that fast. Better yet, she wondered how long the cop had been following behind her. Quickly she threw the bottle of Boones behind the passenger seat praying that it would not break so the car would not reek of alcohol. This was the last thing Anne needed. Another speeding ticket or even worse, a DWI all because she was trying to see Eric's ass. The policeman in the car behind her had his siren on now.

"Fuck," Anne said. "All right, all right. I'm getting over." She put the Styrofoam cup in the cup holder. There was nothing but ice in the cup now. She put her blinker on to signal to the cop that she was going to pull over. As soon as she got into the next lane, the cop car zoomed past her, and the cop was shaking his index finger at her.

"I'll be goddamn," Anne said. Apparently, the cop had more important business to attend to other than Anne going 25 mph over the limit. But he knew damn well she was speeding. That's what the shaking finger meant. It also meant that if he had the time, he surely would have pulled her ass over and written her a fat yellow one.

Anne exited the highway. Driving down the long dark road, she was thinking that Eric better be damn good tonight because she almost went to jail for it. She reached his house. Cynthia had taken the 'Lac just like Eric had said and his 1970 blue Caprice Classic was parked in the drive. Anne pulled up on the curb on the side of the house and turned the engine off. She put on the light within the car to take one last look at herself. Most of the iced mocha lipstick she was wearing had been transferred to the straw from which she had been drinking. She quickly hunted through her purse for the lipstick. She retouched her lips, closed her purse, grabbed the bottle of Boones from behind the passenger seat, turned out the light, and excitedly walked to Eric's door. It had been two weeks since she'd seen him, and her body was calling for him.

She knocked on the screen door. It was so dark that she couldn't see whether there was a doorbell. He was probably asleep. Through the window next to the door, Anne could see the dim glow of a lamp. It looked as though all the other lights were off. She could hear faintly R-Kelly's "Down Low" coming from the CD player inside. She was about to knock again but hesitated when she saw Eric's long enticing silhouette through the window. Anne dropped her keys on the doorstep. As she bent down to pick them up, Eric opened the door. Anne looked up at him. Unsurprisingly, he was butt naked and her eyes were filled with sixty-four inches of rippling mahogany.

✿ ✿

"Hey, babe," Stephanie said to her husband as she bolted through the door.

"How was your night?"

"Fine," she replied as she pecked him on the lips, flung her purse on the couch, and dashed to her bedroom.

"Is that all I get?" Kevin asked, as he threw the remote on the couch and got up to follow Stephanie.

Stephanie was frantically rummaging through her top dresser drawer. There were two old and tattered address books and millions of fragments of papers and napkins with names and numbers on them.

"I'm sorry, babe. I have a very important phone call to make and I can't find the phone number. How are the kids?"

"Sleeping."

"Good. Could you go and check on them for me? As soon as I make this call, I promise I'll apologize to you thoroughly."

"Yeah, yeah, yeah," Kevin responded as he left the room.

Stephanie had sorted through all the fragments in the drawer and still could not find the number. "What the hell did I do with it?" she said to herself.

Stephanie pulled the entire drawer out from the dresser and dumped it upside down. The fragments drifted onto the hard wood floor. One piece of paper with *Cecelia* smudged on it in brown eyeliner pencil landed on top of the pile.

"Found it!" Stephanie shouted.

She rushed over to the phone, dialed the number and sat relieved on the queen-sized bed. The phone rang four times.

"C'mon, c'mon!"

On the sixth ring Cecelia answered the phone laughing.

"Hello?"

"Cecelia?"

"Yeah."

"This is Steph—what the hell took you so long to answer your phone?"

"'Hey, Steph. Girl, me and Cynthia are in the kitchen cooking dinner for the kids. And they're in there with the damn Nintendo up so loud, that Ce and I can barely hear each other speak."

"Oh, good. Cynthia made it there already?"

"Yeah. What's wrong Steph?"

"Nothin. Can I talk to her?"

"Yeah, sure." "Something's wrong," Cecelia whispered to her sister as she handed her the phone.

"What's up, Steph?" Cynthia said.

"Girl, with your dense-ass, you'll never guess."

"Well, what is it?"

"Remember a long time ago I told you that I knew for a fact Eric was cheatin?"

"Look, Steph—don't you start on that shit again. You don't know a goddamn thing. You don't even know the name of the last person you slept with!"

"That would be Gerrard, and I'm gonna prove you wrong, girl. I know for a fuckin fact that your son-of-a-bitch is cheatin! And right now—this very moment is the time for you to find out for yourself—that is, if you really wanna know so that you can get it off your goddamn mind!"

"What the fuck are you talkin about, Steph? You need to mind your own goddamn business."

"Look, Ce. Get your ass up and go home. Right now. Get your ass up and go to your own goddamn house, pronto. Check the couch, the kitchen, the tub, maybe even your own bed—who knows where Eric likes to fuck! Then you'll see what the fuck I mean. But we both know that you already know. You've known for months and have just been denying it cuz you're scared to leave his sorry-ass."

"You need to clean up your own house before you go peekin in somebody else's windows!"

"Just do it, girl."

"Fuck you, Stephanie," Cynthia said.

Stephanie heard could hear the receiver crashing against the wall. Grinning, she hung up the phone.

"Watch it, girl," Cecelia said, picking up her phone. "You wait till you get to your own house before you go breakin shit. What did that nosey heffa say?"

Cynthia was already in the living room grabbing her purse and coat. "Look, can you go ahead and keep 'lil Eric, tonight?"

Cecelia came trailing behind Cynthia and stopped her at the front door. "Yeah, you know I will—what the hell did she say? You know Stephanie's always startin' shit—where the hell are you goin, Cynthia?"

"She said somebody broke into my house. So first I'm going home and if there's nobody there but Eric, then I'm goin to Stephanie's house to jaw her lyin-ass in the face!"

"Jesus! Be careful," Cecelia pleaded as Cynthia slammed the door. She got in her car and was on her way back to Austin.

✿ ✿

"What are you doin down there?" Eric looked at Anne with one eyebrow perched above the rim of his glasses.

"I dropped my car keys. I see you're dressed for the occasion," Anne said, commenting about Eric's attire or lack of it, as she straightened her posture.

"Um-hum. C'mere and give me those lips."

Anne stepped in the doorway and the screen hit her behind and bounced a couple of times before it was still. Eric reached for her waist and pulled Anne hard against him. Her waist was met by his engorged protrusion. His slippery mouth suctioned in her bottom lip so smoothly. Anne sighed. She loved it when he did that. His mouth tasted of Budweiser, which she really didn't care for, but its softness made her forget about it. Eric had always told her that she had some soft-ass lips, but she could not believe that her lips were this soft. It must be Eric's and not her own.

"That's what I'm talkin' about," Eric said. "Bring your sexy ass on in here before somebody sees you standing in my doorway."

"You mean before somebody sees your naked ass in your doorway? What's wrong with you—coming to the door like this? You're liable to make a girl pass out."

Eric laughed and Anne walked on into Eric's house and into the living room. Eric shut the screen door and locked it. He always did this so that in case Cynthia popped up unexpectedly, she would not be able to use her key. Instead, she would have to knock on the raggedy screen door, in which case the entire neighborhood would know that she was home.

Anne placed the Boones on the mantle of the bar and laid her purse down on Eric's creamy white leather love seat, next to his black Guess jeans and Hilfiger shirt which probably had been lying there since he got off at 3:30.

Judging by the outside of the green and white house, you'd never guess that he had such nice furniture inside. She loved his furniture. He and his girlfriend had beautiful shaggy white carpet to match the leather couch and love seat and Anne always wondered how they managed to keep it spotless with a mad three-year-old in the house. She was impressed. They owned a monstrous entertainment center. A big-screened TV sat right in the center, VCR on top, speakers, double cassette player, equalizer and CD player scattered on both sides of beautiful mahogany hard wood, like the color of Eric's skin. It looked as though every button on the entertainment center was turned on. The VCR was on, but the TV was filled with static, and the word *mute* was in the top right corner in fuzzy lime green letters. The coffee table directly in front of the couch had edges trimmed in gold. On top of its glass center were a half empty bottle of Budweiser, an opened box of chicken from KFC, the box for the "Fuck My Black Pussy" flick that Anne knew he had been watching, and a mess of rolling papers. She also knew he had been smoking. But she wasn't going to preach to him about that shit tonight. Besides, he's twenty-six, grown, and he knows what's right and wrong.

Anne stumbled as she walked over to the CD organizer to see which one, she wanted to listen to next. Normally, one cup of

Boones doesn't set into her so quickly, but Anne hadn't had anything to eat since 5:00 and that was over seven hours ago. She picked up CD's by D'Angelo and Gerald Levert. Eric returned to the living room and tiptoed behind Anne. As he cupped both of her breasts with his wide palms and placed his soft lips on her neck, Anne dropped one of the CD's on the floor, startled by his touch.

"Be careful with those, now, cuz those are Ce's. I see you brought some Boones," Eric said.

"Yep, and had some on the way over here, too. Well, in that case—" Anne said, and she purposely dropped the other CD on the floor. She turned around to get a better look at Eric. He wasn't completely naked. He had on a pair of shin-length Nike socks. She stretched up her arms so that she could wrap them around his neck. "Five-0 almost got me tonight," Anne said.

Eric laughed. "You almost got pulled over? Look at cha!"

"Look at me? I was hurrying to get to your ass—" Anne ran one of her hands over Eric's bare buttocks. "—your fine ass."

"What color lipstick is that on your lips? Damn, you got them lined and everything."

"It's called 'Sexy by Anne'," she responded giggling.

"Yeah, whatever," Eric said. "It sure looks good."

"Are you sure that Ce will be gone all weekend or all night, at the least?" Anne was always apprehensive about being in another woman's house, especially when she was about to tear her man up.

"Yeah, I called her to be sure right after we got off the phone earlier." Eric unzipped the back of Anne's sleek silk emerald green dress. His long fingers glided down the indentation of her spine. "Why do you call her 'Ce'? You act like you actually know her."

"You call her 'Ce'. Oh, I guess I'm not privileged enough. Why don't you call me over here one night when she's at home so that I can actually know her?" Anne quivered.

Eric laughed deeply this time. "You're crazy, girl! And ya know somethin? You are doin far too much talking right now."

Eric smothered Anne's response with his moist lips. He kissed her for a long time. Afterward, all Anne could do was smile because he knew, as well as she did, that she had a smart remark to make, but he shut her up with his kiss. Fiercely, Eric lifted Anne's dress over her head, elevating her long mane. She barely had enough time to raise her arms. Her dusty-brown hair floated back onto her shoulders. Eric threw her dress over to the love seat. Then all his movement suspended, as he paused, gaping at Anne.

"Goddamn," Eric said, overwhelmed at what he was seeing. "What do you have on, girl?"

Anne had on an emerald green satin push-up bra that magnified the swelling of her 36C breasts, as it's low cut landed just above her nipples. She wore a little green satin thong to match. She knew that green was Eric's favorite color. The waist of the thong lingered just below her navel ring on her firm abdomen.

"Do you like it?" Anne asked as she laughed. She knew that he did, and she was proud of the response she got from Eric.

"I don't know," Eric denied, a little embarrassed now because he realized he was gawking at her. "Turn around and let me see."

Anne whirled around to show off her big round buttocks. She had a tattoo of a pair of scarlet red lips on her right cheek, just short of the point where the satin thong was engulfed between both of them. Eric didn't lay a hand on her, but Anne felt his warm breath and thin lips whisper against her tattoo. While turned away from him, Anne noticed that Eric had left a glass of Boones for her on the coffee table. He knew by now that she despised beer.

"How sweet," she said, and without looking at Eric, she sauntered over to the coffee table, finished the alcohol all in one swallow and set the empty goblet back on the glass tabletop. She looked up at Eric and stood there in her green platform shoes, bra and thong, with one hand on the curve of her waist, smiling at him. Eric placed his glasses on top of the entertainment center. He bent down and took off his socks and started to approach Anne.

"Wait a minute," Anne said, as she sat down casually on the white leather. She was so used to wearing thongs, that she had forgotten she was wearing one until her bare cheeks touched the cool white leather. "Before you come over here, put in Prince's 'Do Me Baby'. Put it on repeat."

Eric did as Anne requested. He turned off the TV and the VCR, leaving the flick inside the machine. The only light was from the lamp on the other mahogany table. With his erection leading the way, he walked over to Anne, grabbed her by the waist and hoisted her right off the couch. She wrapped her arms around his neck and while still suspended in his arms, she nonchalantly kicked off her shoes, and coiled her legs around Eric's waist. Normally, Anne would have fought viciously to avoid having sex in Eric's living room. There were pictures of him and Cynthia everywhere—the bar mantle, bookshelf, walls, tables. She didn't wanna have to look at Cynthia while she fucked her boyfriend. It was too late now, though. Anne wasn't about to ask Eric to move one thing.

"You smell so good Anne."

Still embracing Anne, Eric turned around and sat on the couch, setting Anne down on top of him. He cupped Anne's breasts in his hands again and kissed the swell of one of them.

"Perfect," Eric said. "Just perfect." Then he kissed the other one. He fondled her back until he found the hooks for the push-up bra. He unhooked it and threw it to the love seat on top of her silk dress. Her breasts bobbed before him; their firmness revealed. Eric enclosed his mouth over Anne's erect nipple. She moaned with desire, and she tilted back her head as Eric licked a pathway on her skin from her breast to her chest, and neck to find her mouth again. Anne kissed Eric once more and then arose from him to slide off her thong. Anne turned around and squatted before Eric. With her hand, she found his erection. She sat down on it, her back facing his chest, as if she were sitting on someone's lap. With his palms, Eric massaged the inside of Anne's thighs. Her hips moved vigorously on the crown of his erection, clockwise, then up and down. Anne looked down at Eric's long toes just in time to see them curl.

"Stop," Eric said, as he opened his eyes and let out a deep breath. "Shit. Stop!"

Immediately, Anne stopped moving.

"What's the matter?"

"It's feeling too damn good. Turn around."

Anne arose from Eric's lap and turned around to face him. She straddled her legs across his lap, knees embedded in the white leather and slid down on his erection again. Eric began to move deep inside of her. Anne kissed three beads of sweat from his forehead. She bent down to find his nipple and her tongue stroked circles around it. Eric clasped his hands on Anne's ass and began to move her on and off his erection even quicker. Anne lifted her head from his chest to his ear. She tickled his right ear lobe with her tongue while she toyed with the other one with her thin fingers. Still grasping Anne's ass, Eric slowed down his movement dramatically.

"Why are you so wet?"

"This is what you do to me," Anne exhaled.

Eric propelled his erection further into Anne's softness.

"Talk to me, Anne."

Her entire body flinched. "I don't know what to say," Anne squealed. She raised her hands from his ear lobes and clasped them both on Eric's head, fore arms mashed against his ears, and elbows nailed into the curve of his neck. Eric's hips thrust his erection into Anne's most impenetrable place.

"Aah, Eric."

"Talk to me, Anne."

"I can't, " Anne desperately blurted out as she opened her eyes. The sweat she had kissed from Eric's forehead had reappeared. She could feel his heart racing in her breast.

"Talk to me, Anne. Talk to me. Anne—talk to me—talk to me—shit—talktome, talktome, talktometalktometalktometalktome..."

Anne looked up at the wall in front of her face. She saw an 8 x 10 of Cynthia smiling down at her. Anne looked right into Cynthia's eyes and smiled back as she closed her eyes and caressed Eric's head of curly hair.

"Eric," she moaned.

❀ ❀

Cynthia had the radio turned all the way up, hoping she could drown herself in the music and wash away thoughts of her boyfriend with another woman.

"That low down son-of-a-bitch!" Cynthia said as she exited the highway going east. She was so angry that she had cried most of the way back to Austin. Even if Eric was cheating, she could not believe he was bold enough to have some hoe in her house.

"That is my mothafuckin house," Cynthia yelled. "I live there."

She sped down the bumpy long road. Her eyes were a foggy red. Her tears formed stains in the makeup on her cheeks. The drops left random spots of brown on her creme blouse from mixing with her chestnut facial powder.

"I will kick his fuckin ass if he has some bitch in my bed. I swear to God I will take his son, and he will never see him again!"

Cynthia rolled over the curb of her driveway and bumped her head on the roof of the car as she pulled into the driveway. "Shit!" she said aloud.

The living room window was directly in front of the driveway. The head lights from the maroon Cadillac beamed through the sheer white curtains. Cynthia slammed on the brakes just short of crashing the car through the window.

✸ ✸

Anne and Eric had fallen asleep naked on the white leather couch. Eric's long body extended the entire length of the couch. His head rested on one arm rest and his feet were crossed over the other. Anne was curled up beside him, one leg tucked into the crack of the couch, the other leg bent lightly across Eric's thigh. Her head was lying on his chest, hair feathered over his shoulder, arm draped casually over his waist, and hand dangling limply off the couch. Both were snoring; Eric louder than Anne. Prince's "Do Me Baby" still going on the CD player.

Cynthia grabbed her Dooney bag purse and got out of the car leaving the radio blasting and the headlights shining through the window. She squeezed between the car bumper and the window to look inside to see who was in the house. She could faintly hear the CD player. She could see Eric's silhouette stretched on the couch, but she could not see Anne's.

She put her purse on her shoulder and turned the latch on the screen door. The latch didn't budge.

"You smart fucker!" Anne yelled.

She forcibly tugged on the screen door. Her purse slipped off her shoulder. She yanked the screen forward so hard it looked like it was going to become unhinged. To make sure Eric heard her outside, she banged the screen on the door seven times with her purse slamming the screen sounding like an echo in response to every tug.

"Open up this fuckin door!"

Neither Anne nor Eric heard the crashing of the screen. Anne had been drinking. Eric had been smoking and drinking, and they both were sleeping heavily now. The Cadillac headlights beaming through the window and across Eric's face finally penetrated his eyelids.

Alarmed, Eric sat right up in the couch knocking Anne's head off his shoulder and onto the cushion. He looked to the window and saw the Cadillac headlights shining on him. Quickly, he ducked back down.

"Fuck! Anne, get up! Get Up! No—I mean, get down. Stay down. If she looks in the window, she can see you."

Cynthia kicked the screen. She walked back to the window to look inside. Eric had lain back down on the couch so Cynthia would think he was still asleep. Cynthia rapped on the window with her keys leaving scratches on the glass.

"O-pen-the-god-damn-door! I know you're in there!"

Eric put his hands over his face. "I can't believe this shit is happening," he said.

"Is Cynthia really out there?" Anne asked as she lifted her head smiling. The idea of getting caught now was turning her on.

"Put yo head down! Look Anne—if you don't get out of here Ce's gonna beat your ass and mine."

"Well, in that case, let Ms. Cynthia on in here—we'll see whose ass gets beat!" Anne giggled.

"E-ric!" Cynthia screamed, still looking into the window.

"I'm not bullshittin," Eric said to Anne.

Eric finally sat up and swung his legs onto the carpet. Quickly he scanned the living room to see where Anne's clothes had landed. Her purse, green dress and bra were all on the leather love seat. Her thong was beside his left foot. One of her platform shoes was next to the stool at the bar. He did not see where the other one was.

"Is that you, Ce?" asked Eric pretending that he'd just awakened and had no idea of who was at the door.

"I'm sure not your mama! Open the door, mothafucker."

"Gimme a minute, Ce. I gotta put some shorts on." Cynthia knew that Eric liked to walk around the house naked, so it wasn't a surprise to her that he didn't have any shorts on now.

Cynthia walked back to the screen door and started pounding it again.

Hastily, Eric got up from the couch. "Don't you move—yet." he ordered Anne.

In one continuous movement, he gathered Anne's purse, bra, thong, shoe, and dress and chunked them in her lap.

"Put your dress on now, and I'll let you out the patio."

"Have you lost your damn mind?" Anne asked Eric as she slipped the dress over her head while still seated on the couch. "Your pitbull is back there. There's no way in hell I'm going out that way. Your ass will just have ta be caught."

"Yeah, yeah, you're right."

"What the fuck are you doin, Eric?" Cynthia yelled into the door.

"I said I was comin, Ce—hold on, alright!" Eric yelled back to Cynthia.

"C'mon!" Eric said. He grabbed Anne by the wrist and jerked her off the couch. She clasped her underclothes, purse and shoe just before they hit the floor. "I'll boost you out the bathroom window. You'll be out on the side that your car is on."

"The bathroom window! What?" Anne asked shocked.

The bathroom window was embedded into the upper wall of the shower. Without turning on the light, Eric stepped into the shower and opened the window. "Gimme your stuff," Eric said.

Anne stuffed her underclothes into her purse. Eric snatched the purse and shoe and threw them outside.

"I'm sorry Anne," Eric said as he grabbed her by the waist, hoisted her to his shoulders and shoved her out the window.

"Mothafu—"Anne said as she hit the cold ground.

Eric grabbed his boxers from the couch, put them on and opened the front door.

"Hey, babe," Eric said to Cynthia unlocking the screen. "What are you doin back so—"

Cynthia exploded through the door, whacked Eric in the face with her Dooney bag purse and rammed him out of her way. Immediately, Cynthia went to her bedroom.

"Have you gone fuckin mad," Eric asked stunned, holding the left side of his face where the purse hit.

"Where the hell is she!" Cynthia yelled.

"Where is who? What are you talking about?" Eric asked trying to play it off. He walked back into the living room to see if he could find Anne's other shoe. "Shit," he said as he spotted it underneath the coffee table. He also noticed Anne's car keys on the floor beside the love seat. Eric dove to the floor and picked up the shoe and keys.

"Where is that heffa!" Cynthia cried. She flung open her closet door and ran her arm against every piece of clothing in there to make sure no one was hiding. She dropped to her knees and peered under the bed. Without a minute to spare, she checked Eric Jr's room, looked in his closet and under his bed. She had burst into tears by now.

"You sorry mothafucka. I know she was here!" Cynthia said to Eric as she proceeded to check every closet in the house, the bathroom, even the garage. Frantically, Eric was trying to think of what to do with Anne's shoe and keys. He heard Cynthia coming back his way and stood straight up with the shoe and keys behind his back. Not even looking at Eric, Cynthia went into the kitchen. With Cynthia in the kitchen, Eric raced to the bathroom and threw out Anne's shoe and keys. He shut the window and tiptoed back up the hallway. He stood with his head leaned against the wall and his hand touching his face where Cynthia hit him with her purse.

"There's no one here but me, Ce," Eric said.

"Shut up!" Cynthia shrieked.

She shut the pantry door and walked to the center of the living room, scanning it for any clues. She finally realized what was playing on the CD.

"Why the hell are you playin 'Do Me Baby'?"

"You know I like Prince, Ce," Eric said, calmly walking to the living room.

Cynthia collapsed on the couch. She saw the empty glass on the coffee table. Her eyes darted to the bar. "Boones?" Cynthia asked. "What's the fuckin occasion?"

"Damn, Ce! I was just chillin," Eric said as he sat down next to her, but not too close because he could see that she was still clenching her purse.

"What took you so fuckin long to answer the door?"

"I was chillin' alone—by myself—solo. You know you do the same thing when I have 'lil Eric and you're here alone. I was smokin' and drinkin', and I passed out. You scared the shit out of me, bangin on that door. I woke up and didn't know what was goin on. Last I knew, you were with Cecelia in Elgin."

"I know, I know. You're right," Cynthia said sobbing as she leaned over and rested her head on Eric's bare shoulder. "I'm sorry I hit you."

Eric slipped the purse handle from Cynthia's hand and placed it on the opposite side of his body, out of her reach.

❀ ❀

Anne was able to hear the ruckus Cynthia caused all the way to the curb where her car was parked. She fumbled through her purse for her keys. "I'll be damn," she said as she realized she never put them back into her purse. She dumped the contents of her purse onto the hood of her Tercel.

"Damn." Anne said aloud. The keys were probably still in the house, if they didn't fall in the grass when Eric booted her out the window.

Anne's sleek, green silk dress was wrinkled now with dirt stains on it. Good thing it's already green, she thought or else there'd be grass stains too. She put everything back inside her purse and zipped the back of her dress.

"This is just great," Anne said talking to herself. "A fucked-up dress, no keys and one fuckin shoe. Was it really worth it, Anne?"

She put on her one shoe, grabbed her purse and hobbled away from her car to the 7-Eleven caddy-corner to Eric's house. When she walked inside the store, the clerk just stared at her.

"What the fuck are you lookin at," Anne grunted. She rummaged through her purse again to get a quarter to call Felicia to come get her. She dialed Felicia's number and the answering machine came on. Felicia's probably gettin her fuck on Anne thought to herself. She hung up the phone, picked up again to call Renada.

"Fuck it," she said, slamming the receiver back onto the wall. Anne decided that she didn't want any of her friends to see her like this. She didn't want them looking at her like the clerk had and asking her what the hell had happened. She dug out another quarter and called a cab. The pay phone was right against the store window. She peered through it. She could still see Eric's house. She could still see his long silhouette through the window. Suddenly, the light from the lamp in the house went out.

Closer than Eric's house, Anne could see her own reflection in the 7-Eleven window. Her dress was dirt-stained and wrinkled. The side of her shin was scrapped and bleeding slightly. She was wearing only one shoe. She didn't have any polish on her toenails, and she could see soil underneath her them. She knew that bottom of her foot was black from walking bare on the pavement. Her knotted, dusty-brown mane had a small yellow leaf stuck in it along with tangles of sun-dried blades of grass. There was a huge purple oval on her neck where Eric had kissed her so hard that blood had risen to the surface of her skin. One of her earrings dangled out of her ear; she could tell that she had lost the back to it. Her mascara had been smeared on her eyelids. Her eyeliner had mixed with the fluids in her eyes and was now clumped in the corners of them.

"Yellow Checker cab, can you hold please?"

"Why not," Anne said. Annoyed by her appearance, she looked past her reflection and gazed at Eric's house through the 7-Eleven window.

She didn't feel very cute anymore.

leave a message

leave a message
when you call
so I'll know it's
you and I'll know
that you think of
me too. and then
I can call you back.
how else will I
know it's you?
unless that's part
of your game. if so,
you should be
shame because
we're too old for that.

airport anticipation

As I sit here
in this blue chair
my heart is racing.
I inhale slow, deep.
I exhale slow, deep,
Staring at the corridor
as people walk through.
One by one, in two's, couples
White shirt, suit, long sleeves,
short, tall…..
Which one will be you and
What will you look like and
What will you do when
You see me?
A kiss? Hug? Smile?
Cry?
And what will I do when
I see you?

my rhythm and your rhyme

My rhythm and your rhyme
makes me whine
it's divine
it's like wine
getting better when you
getting better when we
go slow, so smooth

My rhythm and your rhyme
so raw, pulsing
all up in my behind
please press rewind
let's go again
getting better when I
getting better when we
go fast, go rough

My rhythm and your rhyme
together defeat time
together we dine
on each other
getting better when you
getting better when I
love hard, love deep.

i have this craving

I have this craving
So deep it's beneath
my skin
Flowing
beneath my skin
up and down
from my head
swooping down
and crashing against
the tips of my toes
only to ricochet
sweeping back
through my calves
my kneecaps
my thighs, hips
my
my, my, my
my
navel
my belly
my breasts
plunging over the cliffs
of my shoulders
pounding against my
fingertips
bouncing upward
through my elbows
climbing over my shoulders
up my neck
crawling through my chin, lips,
cheeks, eyes

swarming inside my face
swelling the top of my head
until it ruptures through my scalp
and gushes out
streaming over me
spiraling down, down
coiling around and around
and around my body to
envelop me
closely
smother me
slowly
swallow me
totally
devour me
wholly
shit…..

passion lost

I don't want to be alone tonight
I need to be touched, to be held, to be talked to
The way you spoke to, held, and touched me
Back then.
Even if we have to pretend.
I'd drive the ninety miles at two in the a.m.
It doesn't matter
I just need to see you tonight.
I heard it in your voice that you needed me too, but
You asked me if we could do this another time.
Can you put spontaneity on a calendar?
I guess you couldn't taste my lips kissing yours
Couldn't absorb the warmth of my palms on your skin
Maybe I couldn't make my tones sound desperate
Enough.
Maybe you just didn't understand.

you still look good

"You still look good."
"Can I have a hug?"
"Yes."
We stand up.
Soft hard breath on my neck
Embrace
our lips tightly.
Broad hands molding the
curve in my waist, curve of my rear
Warmth drips dangerously down
the length of my thigh
skirt collapses on the floor
I go up
bounce down on the bed
Get on top
Tears roll down.
I'm so glad I came.
"It was nice seeing you.
Call you sometime."

less is more

less is more;
more or less.
the more I say,
the less you hear;
the less you say,
the more I want you;
the more I complain,
the less you give;
the less you give,
the more I complain;
the less I want you,
the more you give;
the more you give,
the more I want you;
the more you take
the less I have;
the less I have,
the more I need you;
more is less;
more or less,
give or take.

three

"Silence the angry man with love. Silence the ill-natured man with kindness. Silence the miser with generosity. Silence the liar with truth."

— BUDDHA

silence of my truth

loath to ration a
reality, unsure of
its full acceptance

i had heard of tales

Exhausted, I got into my car anticipating the long drive home. Something about the darkness broken only by random streetlights and head lights, the long, loneliness of the highway made the drive home from work soothing, like a glass of wine before bedtime. I drove down the highway south, listening to oldies on KJCE but paying more attention to my thoughts than the cars that passed by me. I was going about 62 in the far-left lane, and I was approaching a car at what seemed like warp speed compared to the other car. Using my peripheral vision, I could tell there was some fool driving at my exact speed in the middle lane, and when I turned to look at him, he was smiling at me. I couldn't get over. I turned to the road again, still going 62 miles per hour and that slow-moving car was immediately in front of me. I had begun to think that it wasn't moving at all. My exhaustion made it hard for me distinguish the difference. Quickly, I looked over my right shoulder again to see if it was clear to merge to the middle lane. That fool of a driver, not realizing the critical situation I was in, was still there, driving at my exact speed, smiling at me. This time I noticed his friend leaning over smiling at me, too. Those assholes were racing me. Or they thought I was racing them. I looked ahead of me again. That slow-moving car was one cars-length ahead of me. I had given myself no time to stop because I was counting on those fools to pass me so I could change lanes. Desperately, I looked over my shoulder. Those fools were still beside me. I gripped my steering wheel, closed my eyes, and swerved hard to the right. I heard and felt a bang on the left side of my car. The instant before I swerved, those two fools sped off. I heard a crash behind me.

The car that was driving behind me rear-ended the slow-moving car ahead of me that I swerved to miss. I was still driving 62 miles an hour. I slowed down and then pulled over to the shoulder on the left of the highway. By the time I came to a complete stop, I was several feet away from the accident. I put my emergency lights on and got out of my car to see if anyone involved was injured and to find out what actually happened.

While I was walking on the shoulder beside the fast lane, an eighteen-wheeler truck came racing past me at 65 miles an hour. The force of the truck as it passed made my entire body sway to the right, and I almost lost my balance. Immediately I stepped off the concrete shoulder and walked the rest of the way on the grassy median.

At the accident scene, there was the slow-moving, red, four-door Nissan Stanza on the grassy median with two Hispanic men standing beside it. There was a white man and woman standing beside a blue Honda on the highway shoulder. Two other white men dodged cars as they ran across three highway lanes to get to the crash scene. The man that was standing next to the Honda started walking toward me. This man, the two white men from across the highway and I all met at the same time.

"I was the first car to swerve. What happened? Are you all right?" I asked the man driving the Honda that rear-ended the slow-moving Nissan. He looked dazed and confused and didn't answer. One of the two men that ran across the highway said that he would go and call the police for us. Then both dashed back across the highway.

I didn't quite know what to do. I had never been in an accident before. I didn't know if I was responsible for the collision of the Nissan and Honda. I didn't know what to say or do and apparently the Honda man didn't either because he said nothing. So, I, out of awkwardness turned around and walked back to my car.

I lived with my parents and every night I worked until 11:30 and got home around midnight. My parents were used to me getting home from work at the same time every night. I didn't want them to worry so I got in my car and went to the nearest pay phone to let them know what happened, that I was all right, and that I'll be home soon.

I took William Cannon, the nearest exit, and drove to the first establishment I saw. I drove around a Wendy's looking for a phone. There was none outside, and the dining area was closed. Then it hit me that I never looked at my car for damage, and I remembered the bang I'd heard on the left side of my car. I got out and walked around my car inspecting it for damage. There was none except a cracked mirror on the driver's side. I got back in my car and drove back to the scene.

When the accident happened, I had been driving on South IH-35. To get back to the scene, I had to turn around on the overpass, get on North IH-35, exit Ben White, go through the turnaround, and get back on South IH-35.

Once back on the highway, I got over into the fast lane because the scene of the accident was on the far-left highway shoulder. I could see lights from police cars flashing. Cars were racing past me, but I had to start slowing down so that I could pull over once I got to the accident scene. I was scared to drive really slow in the fast lane because that's how this whole adventure had begun in the first place, and I didn't want another accident to occur tonight.

So, I put my emergency lights and my left blinker on so that cars behind me would know that something was going on with me and that I was about to get over on the left shoulder. As I neared the accident scene, I noticed a police officer walking on the left shoulder of the highway inside the yellow line with a flashlight raised above his head shining down on the concrete of the shoulder. He appeared to either be getting an estimate of distance by using his feet or looking for something on the concrete. I slowed down even more to about 15 miles an hour. Now at the scene with the red Nissan and blue Honda were that one officer walking the shoulder, and two police cars parked on the grassy median with lights flashing. I pulled over on the shoulder and let my car roll a few feet further into the grassy median so, I wouldn't be so close the fast lane or the accident scene. I left my emergency lights on, got out and started walking once again down the dangerous shoulder to the accident scene.

As I neared the scene, I could see yet another police officer approaching me. When we got to speaking distance, he asked me who I was. I told him my name, that I was the first car to swerve in the accident, and that I left the scene to make a phone call. He gave me a nod in agreement, and he walked beside me over to where the white man and woman, the owners of the blue Honda, and I'm assuming, a couple, were standing.

The woman looked very relieved to see me.

"I'm glad you came back," she said.

"Oh, I was definitely coming back. I had to make a phone call."

The officer that I'd passed walking inside the yellow line was now approaching the other officer, the couple, and I. He walked directly up to me with flashlight shining in my face.

"Don't you know you almost knocked the shit out of me back there! Didn't you see me back there? Don't you know that when you see a police officer you're supposed to slow down! You were driving too goddamn fast!" He was so close to me, so far into my face that I could feel his flying spit hit my face as he spoke. He was so close that I had to take a step back.

I was completely shocked. I had never had any confrontations with the police. I had never personally witnessed an officer behave so angrily, disrespectfully, and unprofessionally. I had always heard tales of angry cops and cops with prejudices and racist cops and violent cops and cops with grudges—all tales that I knew are true. I had always heard of tales of police brutality—tales that I knew were nonfiction. I have had conversations with police officers when I've been stopped in the past. But never in my twenty-two years had I experienced this kind of profane attitude from an officer. And although I knew that bad, violent, racist cops were out there, I also knew that good ones exist, too, and I had always maintained a respect for the law because I knew that law enforcement was a tough field, one that I could never go into. I had always maintained a respect for officers of the law—always until this night.

"I was nowhere near you! I saw you, and I slowed down. There was no way I could have hit you—you were walking inside the yellow line, and I wasn't driving inside the yellow line!" I was so angry I had begun to shake. His unprofessional approach had, in fact, gotten a rise out of me.

"You almost knocked the shit out of me! And you're not supposed to approach the scene of an accident anyway!"

This officer and I were about the same height. I only noticed this because I was so angry that I contemplated fighting this officer. Not a very wise thought, but that only shows how angry I was—so angry that I momentarily thought about risking my life to fight this man. With every word this officer spoke, he leaned into me to intimidate me, still spitting on me, with a red face. By this time the other officer, the one who first approached me, just turned and walked away as if he didn't see or hear what was going on. The couple looked just as appalled as I felt, but they said nothing. They looked as though they had the deepest sympathy for me while, at the same time, they had relief that they were not me. They had backed away, too, and were in the background now.

This officer approached me yelling and very irate so, naturally I reacted and responded to him in the same manner. We were both yelling now.

"You are way out of line! You have no right speaking to me this way. What is your name and badge number?"

"4265553KAYBAB," he flung the information out so rapidly that I was unable to comprehend it. "Now, who are you? What's your name?! Huh? What's your name, what's your name, WHAT'S *YOUR* NAME?!!"

"My name is Smith!" Shouting, I volunteered my address as well.

"WHERE'S YOUR DRIVER'S LICENSE?!"

"It's in my purse in my car. I can go and get it if you like."

"YEAH—YOU GO GET IT!"

He walked behind me to my car. This officer continued yelling and making various thoughtless remarks pertaining to the fact that in his demented mind I had almost knocked the shit out of him, still yelling, still cursing, and still acting as though he weren't wearing a badge.

"You know, I'm gonna write your name and badge number down again because you are way out of line," I said as I opened the door to my car. I grabbed my purse and sat down on the driver's seat with the door open and legs out of the car.

"Fine! Write my name down! You almost knocked the shit out of me!"

"You are way out of line! I am a victim in this situation! I didn't do anything wrong! I'm driving home from work, and I almost had a fucking accident. I was the first person to swerve. I came back here to help!"

"I DON'T CARE!"

"I don't deserve this from you! Your job is to help me—my tax dollars pay your salary!"

"SO! I PAY MY OWN SALARY!"

This is the kind of officer I was dealing with. We both knew that he did not pay his own salary. But he was so irate and irrational that he couldn't think about what he was saying or doing. The whole while we were yelling, I was searching my purse for a pencil and something to write on. Finally, I'd found both.

With pencil and paper in hand I said, "Now what's your name and badge number again?"

"That's it! You're under arrest!"

This officer grabbed me by the arm and yanked me off the seat and out of my car. Out of nowhere a third officer, a female officer, appeared. She turned me around, pushed me on top of my own car and put handcuffs on me.

Those three words were like a blow to my head. I felt as though I were unconscious, as though nothing was real anymore, like I was in a surreal state. I had never in my life done anything to deserve to hear three words spoken to me. I had made a conscious decision to live my life honestly so that I would never have to hear those words. And yet, I was hearing them anyway.

I was astonished. I was angry. I was shaking. I was yelling. I was even cursing now just as the officer was. I was yelling, screaming, cursing anything that came to mind. I was speaking in an uncontrollable rage, trying to make them hear me, hear that I had done nothing wrong, that they had overstepped their bounds.

"Get off me! I'm gonna fucking sue! That's right! I'm gonna sue!"

"Settle down now," the female officer said.

"Settle down? Where the hell were you when he was harassing me?!"

"I don't know where I was, I didn't see that."

Still against my car, I felt the hard handcuffs being clamped around my wrist.

With those handcuffs on, although I knew I had done nothing wrong, I began to feel embarrassed, leaning there against my own car, out in public with so many cars passing by on the highway. So many cars, so many people that must have seen me there in those handcuffs being arrested. So many people looking at me, thinking I was a criminal and thinking that since I was in handcuffs, that I deserved to be in them because naturally I had done something wrong. And I had thought of those who may have passed and seen my brown skin and had already convicted on that fact alone.

Many people that I worked with lived in south Austin and traveled on IH-35 South to get home. I briefly thought of them and if any of them had passed that scene and if any of them had seen me or worse, seen me in handcuffs being arrested. Quickly, I shut those thoughts out of my mind. I had nothing to be ashamed of. I did nothing wrong.

I was shaking; I was scared, but more irate than scared. I was so irate that I felt like crying. I would *not* cry. I would not let that bastard see me cry. Then he would think he had me. I would not give his ass the satisfaction of seeing me cry, seeing me weak. Because that's all it was for him anyway. He wanted control. Control of the situation that he had lost when I asked him who he was and what his badge number was—to identify *himself* to *me*.

At that very moment I thought of tales of people resisting arrest. At that moment I began to understand why those people in the tales may have resisted. At that moment I felt like resisting. And at that moment I wondered if all those people in those tales also resisted because they, like me, had done nothing wrong. I had heard of tales like this, but never would I have imagined that I'd have one to tell.

do you ever?

do you ever feel out of place?
does everyone start out feeling
like they were born to do something
great? can't see your face in a crowd?
scream out loud but you're not heard?
like your life is one big absurd
dream? do you know what I mean?
do you ever feel out of place? like
your life isn't really taking place? like
you can't find that energy to do that
thing that's great? like it's all one
big mistake? look in the mirror and
you can't see your reflection? I
have a confession: I do.

four

"The closer you are to the truth, the more silent you
become inside."

— NAVAL RAVIKANT

silence of pain

I'd rather not give
those who love me the pitty
of seeing me cry.

i stand still

I stand still
when I'm not moving
and I'm not doing
what I should be doing so,
I stand still. Yet,
my mind is always
moving,
thinking of what I
should be doing. Yet
I stand still.
Overwhelmed
by the thought of
choosing a direction
in which to move so, justly
I stand still.

her silence

She's quiet in her feelings. When she goes through things really painful, it's very hard to talk about them. There's almost a certain embarrassment about being in pain. Especially when someone else caused her that pain like in the ending of a relationship. She feels as though the pain she endures is caused by her own blindness, naivety, or even stupidity. She feels that it was her own fault and that others will agree with her, so she keeps it inside and doesn't bother to tell anyone cause she feels they'll say "I told you so" or that they'll feel she should've been smarter in that situation. She keeps these things inside out of embarrassment and out of fear of the responses that others might have. And those responses may make her think that she could have been smarter, that it was truly her own fault that she got hurt—those responses would be an unnecessary affirmation of the way she already feels.

Aside from the embarrassment, going through something painful is hard to discuss because talking about it, hearing the way she feels spoken in words makes the pain harsh and real, like with the illness of a parent. If she doesn't talk about it then sometimes, she can almost ignore it. She can block it out. And sometimes she must. Sometimes that's the only way she can survive. She stays so busy. Her mind is in a million different places all at once. There's no way she can deal with the pain, can't talk about the pain. No time to talk about the pain because talking about the pain would take so much time and would take so much out of her, would make her weak. And there are so many other things that need to be done, and there's no time to be weak. She's got to be strong. Weak people don't survive. Only the strong survive. Talking about pain makes people weak. She's got to be focused, got to keep going, got to get things done. Can't do that and acknowledge the pain, too. So, she blocks it out, so she stays focused, so she keeps going, so she gets things done. She thinks her family thinks she's crazy, that her family doesn't understand her, that her family thinks she's selfish all because she doesn't talk about the pain, doesn't acknowledge the pain. They don't understand that she stays away, stays closed because that's the only way she can deal at this moment. They don't understand that she's fighting so hard to stay strong not only for herself but for them too. She thinks that if she let them in on how much pain she is in that they couldn't deal either. And she thinks that if she tells them—family or friends—about her pains that they will feel sorry for her, sympathize for her, look down on her, ask her to talk about it, tell them about it.

And this is the worst thing of all about dealing with pain. She can't have people feeling sorry for her. In some ways, she wants them to know, she wants them to understand, but she doesn't want their sympathy for her circumstances, for her situation. Having people feel sorry her makes her feel sorry for herself, makes her weak. She doesn't want other people to cry for her, nor with her. When they cry, then she cries, and this is the thing she's trying so hard to avoid. She doesn't want to cry, but when she does, she wants to cry alone. So, no one sees. So, no one knows how deep it goes. So, she can pretend it's not there. And some days she does very well. When the sun is shining bright, and the sky is perfectly blue and the grass is glowing green and she's driving in her car listening to something mellow with the wind blowing in her hair, in her face, she can forget about it completely.

inner peace

I am broke as a spoke
but I'm gonna write a hot check
and still I'm content
My man is away
but this makes me realize how
much I love him so and how
much he loves me
And I'm content.
It's a beautiful day
but all I've done was stay inside and clean, scrub, organize
and still I'm content.
I haven't quite done everything I've wanted to do today
but I have made progress
so I'm content.
I'm overworked and underpaid
but still I always seem to have everything I need,
and then some
so, I am content.
My car needs fixing,
but it's still running
and I'm content.
I've got his awful constant pain in my neck,
but it doesn't keep me from doing what I want to do,
and for this I am thankful and still I am content.
My bills are past due,
creditors calling, mailing.
but the lights are on, cable's on, water running, phone on
and I am content.
I'm not yet the person I want to be,
but I'm young, I'm still learning, and I'm trying
so I am content.

I am sitting in a carwash line so long it's looped around the gas
station,
but the line is moving and I'm
thinking of how content I am
and eventually I'll get my turn,
and I am writing.
I am oh so content.

i see you, brother

I see you, brother.
I look at you and
wonder when
when did we
become strangers?
when did I not know you?
we are so close in age
but so far apart.
we are so much alike
and still so different.
I see pain in your face.
you look like dad now
and all I remember
is the pain in his face
so much to say you have
so much to share you have
intelligence without bounds
but your outlet is not there
I see you frustrated.
I see you scared.
I see you serious.
I want to see you happy,
want to see you laugh
and I want you
to see me, too.

sad song

This song makes me sad—
Makes me remember things
I tried to forget.

repetitively receiving wrongs

When the pain you feel is so real, so deep
but you don't have time to feel it
because you've got stuff to do.
So overwhelmed that crying isn't an option.
When you've been going it alone for so long
that you look up and the support system that you need
isn't there at the very time you need it most.
When you feel the most misunderstood
and the one voice that understands you the most
can't speak for you, can't speak at all because
he's at rest in the Lord.
When what you're needing the most
is to be validated
and you hear crickets.
When you're needing a hug,
open, trustworthy arms to just
collapse in
and there are none there.
When you live your life
Trying, trying, trying
to do the right thing yet
continue to be wronged,
and you pause to ask,
to cry out,
"what am I doing wrong to
receive wrongs
again, and again?"

lovepain

Lovepain is like a sore.
It will heal naturally
with time.
It's when you pick at it
that it remains infectious.
Various events may cause the scab to come off
triggering flashbacks of the lovepain, blood and pus,
but if you look forward and leave the scab alone,
it will heal.
Sometimes the scab leaves a hyper-pigmented scar.
But that scar is an emblem, a trophy, a plaque,
a reminder of a lesson you once learned,
an experience you once had,
a person you once knew,
a thing you once did,
that caused you to feel that lovepain.
And a motivation never to feel that same lovepain again.
But every time, the scar is beautiful.
Beautiful because it makes you uniquely you.
And it produces tough skin, and
a more knowledgeable and stronger you.
And the scars are not accidents.
Each one is where it should be.
The lovepain is Master-planned so you'll
heal a beautifully strong being.
Lovepain is like a sore.
It is an open wound
only if you allow it to be.

five

"Tears are the silent language of grief."

— VOLTAIRE

silence of loss

though I've always been
surrounded by family
I feel abandoned.

last night I dreamed

Last night I dreamed
of licking frozen cups
and eating pralines
and beignets
and pigs lips
and sucking crawfish heads
and sitting on the front porch late at night
rocking in Papa's rocking chair
drinking from his water jar
and eating his good, fat bacon
and sleeping in Granny's brass bed
jumping double-dutch
wearing catholic school uniforms
finding the King cake baby
watching Indians dance and
catching beads and Zulu coconuts
running after ice cream trucks
being bitten by big mosquitoes
and playing the Devil's Eggs
and marbles
and going to Mason Blanche and Picadilly
and eating Granny's sweet potato bread
and loathing turnips over rice
and of being afraid of Brownie and Blackie
and of burning my leg on the green V-dub pipe
and trying not to ride my bike into the potholes
last night I dreamed of my childhood
last night I dreamed of New Orleans.

cooldaddy

cooldaddy, daddycool
with your toe loop sandals
and red bandana around your forehead
blue Farmer Brown overalls
with one strap fastened
cooldaddy, daddycool
suede wine pouch slung over one shoulder
hairy bare-chested and slightly potbellied
upper lining of your silk boxers
creeping out from the waist
cooldaddy, daddycool
with your black aviator glasses
carrying dominoes in one hand
inside your purple Crown Royal bag
cooldaddy, daddycool
hopping on your ten-speed
to get a pack of Kools
or moseying in the Caravan
with old Shadow in the hatch
calling all the women baby
they all call you Smitty
cooldaddy, daddycool
pulling out the brown folding table
to play a hand of Spades
turn on the tape player
to listen to some Maze….
you had us all in a daze
in a maze
ment of your style
your smile
your profile.
that's my cool daddy
yeah, my daddy cool.

lil' cousin

When they told me you were
shot and killed I didn't know
what to feel. I had no tears to
cry for you. I said I felt discon-
nected from you, far away from
you with only vague childhood
memories keeping you in my
reality. so I prayed and asked
god to bring you closer to me.
and when I saw you in that casket
a swole up man and not a silly
scrawny boy, that made it semi
real. I saw it was you but you
weren't there. your soul was
gone, your face was bare. you
were familiar but not the same.
then somebody showed me a
picture of you as a man sitting
on a park bench staring off into
a field. and your face was painted
with that boyish smile, a brilliant
smile. that smile that put the "lil"
in lil cousin and that's what brought
you back to me. your smile is your
spirit and it replaced the empty
inside of me. god allowed me to
remember you. your smile will
shine inside of me eternally and I
don't even need that picture no
more. when I think of you I see
your smile and it fills me. your

smile was your gift from god and
your gift to us. it remains alive
in all who loved you for always.
your smile is what made you
and what will forever keep you
lil cousin. thank you for always
smiling and thank you for making
us smile. rest easy lil cousin.

corrosion

Time is dripping slowly, constantly.

Drops form lines as they slide.
Black is painted over the yellow on the canvas,
that moment framed.
The faucet is still on.
A fresh canvas under the brush is painted,
first yellow, then black.
The lines are sliding more quickly now. More quickly, the brush
strokes—
So quickly there's no time to mount the yellow.
The canvas must be framed.
And black is quicker. Black is darker. Black is solid.
Black is stronger. Black is closer.

The knob squeaked.
The drain swallowed the last drop.
The Masterpiece framed with black lines and
fingerprints of rust are at the heart of the canvas.

dad – change it all to past tense

Now that I think about it, I've never seen my dad rushing. He takes his time about everything, even when he's running late. Maybe his taking his time has much to do with his thoroughness. If you ask him to show you how to play dominoes, he will walk you through the game from start to finish and will even include little helpful hints like always predicting what the opponents have in their hands. When it was time to go to New Orleans for Christmas, all the suitcases had to be packed the night before and no one left in the morning until every cord was pulled from the wall sockets and every window had been double-checked that it was locked.

He is extremely firm in his decisions, like the time I was grounded for wearing his shirt without permission. I had always had a favoritism for men's shirts because they come in much nicer, more colorful prints. I had a habit of taking my dad's shirts and secretly wearing them to school. I say secretly because I had gotten caught before and understood my dad didn't want me wearing his shirts at all. At any rate, I had planned to go a New Edition concert with all my best friends. As a matter of fact, my parents told me I could go to the concert the very night I got busted for wearing my dad's shirt. So, that very night my dad reversed his decision and told me that as a part of my punishment I could not go to the concert. Several weeks passed, and I was still grounded. One of my best friend's dads was a friend of my dad's and he even tried to talk my dad into letting me go the concert because he thought my dad was being too hard on me. My dad was relentless, and I remained grounded while all my friends went off to the New Edition concert.

My dad sometimes uses humor to get important messages across to me. There was a time when several of my checks bounced and almost every day for a week, I received notices from my bank in the mail about the bounced checks and the bank's $25 charge for them. My dad would check the mail and give me the notices. He would say that I must be a part of the "$25-club" and that the bank must love me for it. What he was really saying wa that I should be more careful in my check writing because in the long run I will spend more money paying for bounced checks.

I wish he were still here. I miss his wisdom, his voice, perspective, approach. One day, I'll finish this. I'll have to change it all to past tense.

dear daddy

Dear Daddy,
I remember when you
used to call me "Sticks"
but that doesn't apply anymore.
I remember when you
used to pull my pony tails
straight up in the air.
I was your "Boobie".
I've grown and matured,
but I'll always be your girl.
You taught me that
I'm a lady and that
I shouldn't accept anything
less than to be treated as such.
You taught me to be strong
and independent from any man
or anybody for that matter
and that is a lesson I have learned well.
I've inherited so many traits from you.
I think that's why you and I
clashed at times.
But I've got your work ethic and
stubbornness or "bull headed-ness"
as Mama says,
and these traits have been
a great advantage in my life
and will continue to be
in the future.
I am thankful and
blessed
more than words could

ever say to have a
Daddy
as dedicated, supportive,
and loving as you.
Everything you did was
for the benefit of your family.
I appreciate all that
you've done for me
trampoline lessons,
judo, chess,
that raggedy 3-speed bike,
showing me how to change a flat,
scoping out my male friends,
helping me buy my cars.
Although my heart aches
that you are gone,
I thank God
that I have twenty-three short
but wonderful years of loving
you and receiving love from you.
I love you Daddy.
See you soon.

at the shoreline

A spiraling shoreline
glistening water
eternal sunshine
breezy air
deep blue
feeling cool.

Leaves are cool
floating down the shoreline
staring into blue
thrashing water
in sync with the air
glaring in the sunshine.

bronze sunshine
keeping my mind cool
forget about the air
reflect on the crystals at the shoreline
brought in with the water
and appreciated by the Blue.

Rocks are blue
from the pressing sunshine
kept damp by the water
and cool
all along the shoreline
caressed by air.

Not wind, just air
transcending blue
shaping the shoreline

fed by the sunshine
soothing and cooling
simple water.

Embracing water
and peppery air
enveloping cool
fluorescent blue
hyper sunshine —
all framing the shoreline.

Heavy sadness cools with a thoughtful mind kept moist in the
sunshine.
Something about the shining blue enters me and mixes with my air,
When I'm sitting at the edge of the water, messing with the shells
at the shoreline.

your reflection

I look at your tall frame, long slender legs, narrow feet,
your broad shoulders, the thick veins in your hands and arms,
the line down the center of your thumb,
broad shoulders

I observe your quietness, your stubbornness,
your strong will, your wit, your way of expressing yourself
through actions instead of words,
quietness

I notice your deep, slanted eyes, the smirk in your lips when
you smile, the way you tilt your head in photographs, the sarcasm
you play with at difficult times,
deep, slanted eyes

And I see myself.

every so often i cry for you

Every so often I cry for you
when I'm reminded of how deeply you suffered,
to remind me that you're gone
to remember that you loved me
to show that I love you
to acknowledge that I do hurt
and that it hurts me.

Every so often I cry for you
when it hits me that you knew you would
not walk me down the aisle or see my brother marry
not grow old with your wife
not ever brush Shadow, or get that motorcycle or
that trailer and travel all over, just the two of you
or build that fence, or fix that Volkswagen, or buy that other dog,
teach your grandkids how to fish, play dominoes, chess
not eat pizza, fried chicken, hot sausage again
not play basketball or tennis again
not ever got to Mardi Gras again
not ever see your mother again

And when I realize that you knew you would
not walk very far
and then not walk at all
and not sit up for long
and then not sit up at all
and not talk for long periods of time
and then not talk at all and
not eat very much and
then not eat at all and
not ever get out of that bed, not ever leave the hospital,
see your house again, not ever survive without that tube,

that you would not survive at all.

Every so often I cry for you
when I reflect on how bravely you fought
for us and for you and
I cry because you fought in vain—
God's strength was greater.

Every so often I cry for you
because I know there was so much
you could not express
so much that you kept within
and I know that my life is not the same
that everything is not all right
because I realize that the only reason that I persist
is to rub your soft arm and stroke your fine hair the way
I did at your bedside and
to see your smirk, hear you call my name, to see you pull
the van up into the driveway, see you run, see you walking Shadow,
see you sitting on the bed beside Mama when I come home, to
hear
your boots on the stairs
all again
and to have an instant
a fraction of a second
to embrace you the way we did
when I was your "boo-bootsie",
your little girl
so I could brand your warmth into my skin
so I will never forget the spirit of your love,
to hear once more, "love you, boo."

Every so often I cry for you
or,
do I really cry for me?

six

"Love said to me, there is nothing that is not me. Be silent."

— RUMI

silence of love

complexity of
raw feelings needing actions
authentic and pure

visions of a man

I have visions of a man.
one who understands
holds my hand,
knows when I'm mad,
knows when I'm sad and
feels my pain.
who won't play games,
one who's not in it for gain,
who remains the same,
who will walk through the rain,
and not just through the sunshine.
One who knows rhythm and,
one who knows rhyme.
who does not whine.
who reads my mind,
yet blows it too.
who will say "I love you"
no matter who's around,
who doesn't get around,
who will not clown when
I'm feeling down or
when I want to get down.
I have visions of a man
who walks with dignity,
listens with empathy,
talks with his whole body,
understands with his heart,
knows the art
of two
of him and me.
who knows our history,

and does his damnedest not
to take us back to where we came
from the rain
from the wind
from the storms
of love.
I have visions of a man
sent from up above,
blessed from heaven,
who adores his children,
yet will be stern when
they get out of hand
and knows when to say when,
when I can't say it for myself.
one who knows the steps,
the first through the twelfth
play. you know what I mean,
you know the theme.
I have visions of a man
who opens doors,
yet will still scrub a floor
when it's dirty.
one who will be flirty,
but only with me.
who will take the time
to go through the drill,
feel the thrill
the pleasures of
massage oil,
legs that coil,
fingertips,
strawberries chocolate dipped,
Zifandel,
rose petals pastel,

black lace,
fire place,
purple hot flames,
strokes my mane,
lavender,
mink fur,
T-backs,
aphrodisiacs,
bubble baths,
rubs my calves,
warm honey,
satin nightie,
incense,
sweet fragrance,
candlelight,
pellets of ice,
silk sheets,
soft beats ,
listens to my mind beat.
I have visions of a man,
a Superman,
not a super-natural man.
a super REAL man.
a man who is real,
and is super
in his own right.
one who knows his own might
and his own capabilities.
one who won't let anybody
disrespect me
Or his family.
who will protect me,
stand up for me,
stand beside me,

stand behind me.
I have visions of a man
who sends me flowers,
who will take showers,
with me and wash my hair.
who buys me pretty underwear
and shiny jewelry to wear.
who will be there
when I can't bare
the loads of life.
not Tina and Ike
but Will and Jada
Pinkett-Smith.
who knows that romance
is not a myth,
not a fairytale,
but it is real.
and it lives
and breathes
and burns
in him and me
as long as we be.
I have visions of a man
not who I wish were mine,
but who is mine
until the sands of time
have run out.
that's what this is about.
I have visions
of a man
because
I have seen this man.
I have only just begun to know this man.
I have touched this man,

kissed this man,
supported this man,
adored this man.
I have married this man.
Made love with this man.
I love this man.
He is my man.
My vision.

I used to be a lover of poetry

I used to be a lover of poetry
but now it only irks me
because it seems to be
that it's just for the
melancholy
or the lovelies—
as love lives, love
lies
in poetry.
However, in reality,
lovely love lies in poetry as
my love is never really
how the poem says it should be,
you know, how the poem says it is—
you see, he said I was his,
never mentioned she was his; I thought
these lines were all mine.
He didn't admit I'd have to share his kiss
with this phantom miss, mysteriously
revising our love.

I used to be a lover of poetry
but now I'm just a lover of what used to be,
since seemingly,
my poems were open
to whomever wanted to join him.
("Open call! Come on in!")

I used to be a lover of poetry
because it used to make me want thee;
it used to fill me,

to make me feel lovely love—
nourished. The poetry flourished—
it loved me like there was no she
or me, just we
lying between the lines,
waiting to be spoken out loud,
released from the page
from where we never age,
from where it never gets old.
We were word wine,
and when we were uttered
by the tongues of wine-warmed lovers, we fluttered—
flutter-flew flutterflied,
butterflying across the lines
our story spoken, no matter how many times,
was wine,
uncorked. Words sometimes
unspoken, outspoken,
we were lovely. Savored.

The poetry, though, is where our love lies,
love lived, where love used to be
because now it only irks me. It metastasized,
became a cancer,
used me, transformed—
tricked me
for I found out that
love lies in poetry
the moment I looked into
his eyes
and saw her.

move you up?

"Ma'am?" Having cleared level 69, she looked up from her cell phone and saw him through the rolled-down driver side window, standing just a foot away in the parking garage of the hotel. Curly, unkept hair. Hands in dingy grey sweatshirt pockets, wrinkled black pants, the cold making his breath visible as he exhaled. He must have rushed in to work this morning, she thought, as she sized him up.

"Are you waiting for someone ma'am?"

"Yes, he just went inside to grab something from our room. He'll be right down," she said, reassuringly.

"Can I move you up?" with his head, he motioned at the gap in the temporarily parked cars in front of hers.

Ordinarily, she wouldn't allow such a thing. She glanced again at his unkept clothing, looked at the cars, the glass rotating lobby doors, all the busyness around her and thought, ok.

"Sure."

He hopped in, cupped his hands, and breathed on them, as he settled into the driver's seat of her car.

"Where are y'all headed?" he asked, glancing down at her left hand. He smelled of cigars, oil, onion.

Immediately, she felt uncomfortable. "A football game," she said, trying to sound nonchalant. Cell phone in her right hand, she tucked away her left into her coat pocket, hiding away all six shiny carats that adorned her ring finger. She made certain her purse was zipped and positioned between her feet and tried to act as though she was still into her game app and not at all uneasy.

"This is nice. What year is this?" he asked.

"This year's model." She glanced at her door to make certain the passenger side was still unlocked so she could make a quick exit if necessary.

He put the car in drive. "Y'all from here, ma'am?" he asked.

"No, here just for the weekend." Those words uttered robotically, automatically, and far too quickly. She regretted giving him that information.

He put his foot on the gas, but the car didn't move. He still had his foot on the brake. Pressing the gas, while his foot on the brake made the car rev a bit.

"Sorry. Just wanted to make her moan a bit," he said, grinning at her.

She didn't return the grin, but instead tilted her phone a bit more toward the door, making sure he couldn't see the screen. She left the game app, went to the dial pad, and keyed in 911 but didn't press "call" just yet. Her thumb lingered over the lighted word, just in case.

"No worries," she said, "my husband does that, too." She wanted to remind him that there was a man bound to come out of the hotel at any minute to check on her.

He released the brake and slid the car up two car lengths. He then put the car back in park and cupped his hands again, breathing on them for warmth. She noticed cracked cuticles and dirty, bitten nails.

"Man, this cold came outta nowhere," he said, looking at her.

Fed up with his small talk, she looked him square in the eye, just about to tell him where to go, when she saw him flinch. Her direct eye contact immediately made him look away. He looked down, between her legs, at her purse strap. He couldn't possibly want a tip, she thought.

Her husband kept spare change in the console. Still keeping her thumb poised above "call" on her cell, with her left hand, she opened the console, held it open with her left elbow, fished out a bill, and looked at it. It was a $50. She wanted to put it back before he saw it. She looked up at him. He was already eyeing the bill. She didn't want to give this man $50. He hadn't really done anything to earn this type of tip. She fished around one-handedly a bit more until she got to the bottom of the console, and her fingers found loose change. When the man heard the coins, he started coughing profusely in his hands. Even more anxious and not wanting his germs, she slammed the console down with her elbow.

"Here you go," she said, handing the wrinkled bill to him.

"Oh, no ma'am," he said, his lit-up eyes tracking the bill.

She shrugged her shoulders and just as she was opening the console again to put the bill away, he quickly said, "Well, ok. My mama did teach me to never reject blessings."

"Is that right?" she said with a bit of sarcasm as she put the bill in his grimy hands, tip of tattoo on his inner wrist exposed. Something inked in red.

"Yup. Along with, be kind to strangers. God bless you ma'am. Take care." He swiftly opened the door and hopped out of the car. He swiftly walked toward the back of the car. She pressed the auto windows so that the driver's side one was now up, and she locked the doors. She turned the rear-view mirror toward her, so she could watch him inconspicuously. He walked past the hotel doors and kept walking right past the valet desk. He was headed for the sidewalk.

She looked past him and saw a crowded sidewalk across the busy downtown street. On the corner, in front of the pharmacy, she couldn't spot his dingy sweatshirt. Moving the mirror around some more, she realized it wasn't him. It was a woman, smiling, holding a baby in one hand, the other hand on a stroller handle. Then she thought he came into view as she saw another grey sweatshirt.

A car pulled up behind hers, so she peered through the passenger side mirror instead.

She couldn't remember if he was wearing a name tag. It was him. As he was crossing the street, he waved his right hand and in it, the bill she'd given him flopped about. Then he put it back in his pocket. With excitement, he pounced on the hood of a cab that was stopped at the red light and back to his feet. The driver of the cab blew the horn at him. The cross walk was crowded with pedestrians, but she could see he'd made it to the corner where he embraced, lifted, and twirled around the grey sweat-shirted woman, while she was still holding the baby.

He put her down, put his hand in his pocket.

A city bus driving by stopped to pick up and let off passengers. It blocked her view. Unlocking the doors so she could get out to keep her eye on him, she was startled by a knock on the driver's side window. A white collared valet, with gold trimmed name tag leaning over, was peering through her window. She rolled it back down.

"Park your car, ma'am?"

"No thanks. He'll be right out. I promise."

"No problem, ma'am. Have a good day." She noticed his shoes as he walked away. Black dressy. And pants, creased, spotless.

Just as she was putting up the window again, she heard tires screeching, a loud thud, and several screams.

The city bus still blocked her view. She got out of the car and stood, leaving the car door ajar. She still couldn't see what had happened, but she noticed crowds of people headed toward the intersection.

Car still running in park, and car door ajar, she started walking through the hotel parking garage toward the street. Coming toward her was her husband, limping. Odd. He was supposed to be inside the hotel.

"I'm sorry I took so long," he shouted, approaching her, jogging, limping.

As he got closer, she could see his overcoat torn at the shoulder and pants mud-splattered. "What happened?" she asked, finally face to face, he embraced her tight and long, but didn't answer.

"What happened, love? I heard screams. We should see if we can help."

"You don't want to go out there."

She stepped away from him an arm's length and noticed splashes of red on his white collar. "What happened to you, Carl?" He smelled like onions.

"There's a guy. Might be dead. In the street."

"My, lord! And you?! What happened to you, Carl?" Frustrated that he was taking so long to put the pieces together. He was still out of breath and a bit disillusioned.

"I was leaving the drug store….."

"What were you doing at the drug store?" She cut him off. "You went in the hotel to register us and get directions!"

"I know, I know. Headache. Hotel didn't have Tylenol. Can't take Ibuprofen because of my blood pressure. Thought I'd run across street to get Tylenol."

"Ok. And, the screams, the screeching, the guy?!"

"I was crossing the street and dropped the blasted Tylenol. I bent down to pick it up, and the next thing I know, a guy tackled me to the ground. Then I heard the crash."

"What crash?!"

"Traffic light changed too quickly. I guess the driver of the car didn't see me bent over. This guy shoved me out of the way. The driver couldn't brake in time. Rolled over the guy, I think. Lots of blood. The car ran into the traffic pole, I think."

"Carl!"

He opened his right hand to show her the Tylenol that he'd bought and retrieved from the street.

"We need to go help, Carl!"

"They've already called 911. Some homeless guy, I think. I'm ok. We're going to be late." He was beginning to catch his breath. "I need to take this Tylenol. Everything hurts now."

They heard sirens in the distance.

"Ok, you go sit in the car. I'm going to see if I can help."

He limped to the car and got in on the passenger side.

She made her way through the crowd. "I'm a nurse!" she shouted, lying, so she could get to the victim. The crowd made room for her. There he was. Mangled legs. That familiar sweatshirt, now bloodied. She was about to kneel beside him when an on-looker said, "I'm a doctor, ma'am. He's gone. You know him? She shook her head as she stepped backward. She began looking for the woman with the baby. She was still standing on the corner, in front of the drugstore. Both arms embracing the baby, holding it tightly, the infant's head buried in her bosom. She stood silently crying. She turned to walk back to her car to check on Carl, when she saw the $50 floating in a bloody stream that led to the gutter, when another on-looker rescued it and quickly walked away.

"Hey!" she yelled. She began to run. "Hey, stop!"

Startled, the on-looker simply stopped and turned around. Easily five inches taller than her, the slim pedestrian towered over her. She mustered up all her courage, "Give it to me."

"What?!" he said, offended.

"The bill. Give it," she used her most commanding voice. The one reserved for the most obstinate students.

"You *crazy*," he said.

"That's mine, and you have three seconds to hand it over," she said, she held out her hand with the expectation that he'd place the bill in it.

"You are crazy. Take it," he said, giving it to her and walking away.

She turned around and made her way back to the lady with the baby.

"Ma'am?" the nurse impersonator said.

The lady didn't look up. Her cheek was resting on top the baby's bald head. She caressed the baby's head with one hand, the baby's back with the other.

Ma'am? she asked again. "Do you know the victim?

The sweatshirted lady didn't answer.

"I'm going to put something in your pocket, ok?" She took the $50 and placed it in the sweatshirt pocket. "Are you ok?" She knew that was a dumb question.

Leaving the lady and the infant, she walked across the street through the crowd.

Police were now on the scene. "Anyone know this man?"

"I think she does!" Carl's wife yelled, pointing to the woman, who still didn't look up or lift her cheek from her baby's head.

Following Carl's wife's tip, an officer was making his way to the sweat-shirted woman. Carl's wife headed back to her car to check on Carl.

She found him reclined in the passenger seat, door still ajar. Her purse between his feet.

"Are you ok, Carl? Let's get some ice."

"I wouldn't know where to put it. Everything hurts. Man, I'm out of shape."

"Let's just go and check into our room. The rest can wait."

She reached out her hand to help him up.

"Ma'am?" the valet said. She looked up. "Can we move you up?"

"You can park it," she said.

desperate measures

she wanted u to love
her so she said she loved
u. she wanted u to want
her so she said she was
having ur baby and now
that she got u hooked,
she scared b/c u ain't
playing. and she scared
cuz there really ain't no
baby and she scared
cuz she really don't luv u
although she really don't know
that yet. but sho nuff, she will.
but now that she got u
hooked,
what mo' can she say?
she don't love u and
the baby's gone? she
have to keep on making
up those desperate words
b/c she know u ain't playing
and if u find out u gone take
some desperate measures
too.

i'm sorry

I'm sorry
for when I yell and curse
for not being more expressive
more affectionate
for not paying more attention
for not comforting more
for when I don't understand
for not trying harder to understand.
But know that I'm committed to you
and I'm not going anywhere
and I thank you
for your patience
your sweetness
for loving me still
in spite of all my shortcomings
and I appreciate you and everything you do
and all that you intend to do
and because of this I am committed
to being a
better wife
better lover
better friend
to you.
Even if it takes
the rest of my life.

happy anniversary

my lover, my husband, my friend
here we go again
we made it through another year
keeping each other close and near
I can't hardly believe it's here
just year number three?
it really seems like an eternity
of being with you on this
turbulent ride of love
we really are "lucky" (smile)
that's non-believer-speak—for it really is a "blessing"
that we're still together
now let's see if we can weather
another year of love
however, let's make this one different
a stronger commitment
more heaven-sent
more dignified
a smoother ride
in love
together
we can endure another year
if we both believe
and promise to give and receive
love freely from each other
to understand one another
to forgive one another
and be sweet to each other
that's how we'll arrive at eternity
by not taking each other so seriously
and learning that we can be trusting

once more
my lover, my husband, my friend,
today let's close the door on years before
and let a deeper love begin
so, here we go, but not again,
today we go
anew:
a new me
a new you—
a new we.
happy anniversary.

silently

Silently I fell
Now silently, I walk away.
I didn't know, neither did you.
Am I for sure? When did it happen?
Did it happen when
we used to sit in the car
under the bridge and daze
into the waves,
watching the steam roll over them?
You took me to that place
on my birthday
and threw rocks at the ducks?
We went walking in the park on that trail in the blazing heat?
We lay across the bed and stared out into the clouds?
When you shared your nickname with me?
When I decided I could never see you again?
When we talked on the phone for hours after she left?
When we took long drives in the dark just to get lost?
When you called my name while making love?
I didn't know, neither did you.
When did it happen? I am for sure?
I am sure.
Silently I fell, but
Now silently
I rise.
I walk away.

revealed

always on my mind
yet unavailable,
satisfied, mystified,
specified, tongue tied,
you lied,
terrified, mortified,
hypnotized, desensitized,
dehumanized, demoralized,
realize, I'm not shy,
capitalize,
open your eyes,
surprise

she

When she gets on her soap box
about race relations or romantic relationships
she starts flowing like a river and only a dam will shut her up,
unless she gets her point across first.
She is pretty as a rose in full bloom,
and as sweet and sensuous as a strawberry,
but don't let that fool you—
like a lioness, she will defend her ideas till the death.
She frequently invites us all to congregate under the enveloping
branches of her private weeping willow to eat, drink, play Spades,
chill. If for some reason one us can't make it home,
she lends us her bed; if we need to run an errand,
she lends us her 240x; if we tell her we're hungry,
she'll make us dinner; if we tell her we're cold,
she'll give us her blanket; if we can't pay our way, she'll give us the
money.
Her heart is like the motherland of Africa,
protecting and loving her brothers and sisters,
those close to her and those she doesn't know.
Her desire to free her brothers and sisters from their miseries
and her ability to organize, both like that of Harriet Tubman,
are evident in her relationships with us and in her field of social
work.
She is like black leather—smooth in the way she communicates,
bold when it comes to getting what she wants,
and tough in every meaning of the word.

for my granny on her birthday

Grandmother.
Grand. Mother.
Mother of me.
Mother of them.
Mother of them all.
Grand.   Mother.
Those two words should remain separate
Like grand piano, grand central station, grand finale
And G-R-A-N-D in all caps to be said as if it were yelled
Because it means something more
than our young girls these days would be fortunate to ever tell.
Some say Me-Maw, Nana, Granny, Big Momma, Mama Sue
All the same, we get our skills from you.
Don't think, grand-daughter, that you came here knowing what
you do.
You were trained by your mother
and her by her mother
and her mother by her mother.
It is more than a title—
It is a right. It is a cloak. It is a crown.
And, when She crosses your path, you really should bow down.
For she is the mother of me, and she is the mother of she, my
daughter.
She is the mother of every child that comes after her,
that comes after me.
She is *THE* grandmother.
And she is more than grand. Please understand.
She is great. Gorgeous. Glittery hair. Grandeur. Gracious giver,
glorious womb, glowing, gifted, glamorous, guaranteed lover,
gigantic heart, guided by God, glorified hands in the air, praising
Jesus our God, glory, glory to our God, she is gold.

Halleluiah! Truth be told!
She is—She *IS*,
Thanks be to God.
We won't gloss over all her struggles either.
She conquered them with grace and
Only she knows the inner face
Of what it means to be great, grand,
Grace of God.
For her, we are grateful.
So grateful she is
grand.
So grateful that, through birth, she became grand.
I pray that there is a GRAND in me
That I shall be, shall see, some day.
Her legacy will be born through me
For all generations to see.
I pray that she is me—.
Your grand-daughter.
Love, sincerely,
Me.

rainbow

I saw a rainbow
and it moved me
to think of
you, our time
together. It was a colorful
smile from you. And I
smiled back.

you said

you said you'd always
be there
said you'd always care
I don't dare
to ask where
you are now
because somehow
I knew that you
had to go
it wasn't meant to be
you wouldn't be
with me
you couldn't stay here
I couldn't keep you near
enough
our love wasn't that
tough
and now I miss you
so much
I do care
you said you'd always
be there
you said
you'd always
be
you said.

seven

"If what one has to say is not better than silence, then one should keep silent."

— CONFUCIUS

silence of chaos

when the heart and mind
attempt to reconcile sheer
incompatibles

pictures

Your pictures are a fortress
a dam, a skeleton, a crutch under each arm
There are three on the nightstand: you in your suit,
In your fatigues, in your dressy greens
Three on the shelves: at Fisherman's Wharf,
at McDonalds with matching sweatshirts,
embraced at the top of the stairs.

There are two in my wallet:
You sitting on your black Daytona wearing that vest
I never was sure I liked, your graduation day

But I don't look at any of these.

Yet, I can
envision
each one with the sharpness
and vividness
of one taken moments ago.
And I can
picture
every detail, even the stripes on your sleeve
every detail, except your face.

I don't quite remember what your face looks like
and I refuse to look at the pictures.
Your face, your smile reflects my tears.
Everyone is a snapshot of that night you
dragged me into below freezing weather with intent to
deceive.
I imagine they don't exist, knowing they
surround me.

And still I
cannot take them down from the shelves,
out of the wallet,
off the nightstand.
It's easier
to just keep your pictures
in their places
because that's where they were when
I was sane.

four to one

That concert, that girl and her money, your divorce.
You lied and you lied, and you lied,
and on Christmas Eve, you lied again,
with that message from yet another girl.
Same old topic. Same old lie.
So, on Christmas morning I told you
to drive me home.
Your lies had broken me down
so low, so low, so low, lowest.
Did you have good intent?
Well, you lied.
Was I just tripping?
Well, you lied.
So, on Christmas morning when you pulled into my driveway,
I got out and went inside my house.
You tried to follow
but I don't know why.
You said you had my gift
but I don't know why.
I said, "I don't want it"
You said, "Please take it."
I said. "No, no, no, no."
Still you pushed it through the door crack.
And you stood there.
And you cried.
As if you had just lost your best friend.
Well, you had.
And you knew it.
And you knew it was over.
And you knew you would never see me again.
No more, no more, no more, no more.

You looked at me as if
I wasn't being fair.
You lied and you lied and you lied and you lied.
I shut the door on you only once.
I believe that's more than fair.

i've got your number

I've got your number
You don't do things
you know you should
because you know it'll upset me.
That is your way of keeping me
captive
Keeping me near you
involved with you
Because you know that if I'm thinking
About that silly shit
that bothers me so
then I can't possibly think
of me
or what I need
to be
doing
or whom I need to
become.
Yes, I've got your number.
It's your way of keeping me small
of knocking me down,
of making me know my place,
as I've heard you say
But I tell you today—
That from now on
I will not complain
or obsess about
the small stuff
because I've got places to go.
things to accomplish
that are so much bigger

than this little world of yours,
and these little habits of yours,
that bother me.
and you ought to be ashamed
of your mentality.
I've got your number,
and here's what I will say:
you have responsibilities,
daily,
that you will meet.
Small tasks that are part
of everyday living,
that everyday people do,
that you will do
because I will not do
them for you.
nor will I stand by
and watch you not do
them for yourself.
I've got your number
and
the choice is yours.
You can do them now
with me
or you can do them later
with some body
else.
Either way
I am free.
Believe me
or not.

it does not matter

Today is the 25th and
it does not matter
anymore
what you do
or don't do.
I've told you how I feel
looked you in the face
and said that you hurt
me once
But you won't do it again.
Because what you do
doesn't matter.
And it doesn't matter
because whatever you do
I will survive it
get over it
live on.
So, what if you hurt me again?
It's not your action that hurts;
it's how I feel about your action
that hurts.
And I'm beyond falling for your actions.
So what?
You've hurt me before,
so I won't be surprised if you do it again.
However,
next time I will not dwell on it
So.
What.
So, what if you do this?
So, what if you do that?

What you do does not define me.
I existed before you,
I will exist after you.
So be it if there is a next time.
I'm already at peace with it;
I've already resolved to move on.
Because it just doesn't matter.
Not anymore.

monday thru friday

Monday thru Friday
I am alone
Monday thru Friday
you're not home
Monday thru Friday
I cook and I clean
Monday thru Friday
you're selfish and you're mean
Monday thru Friday
you make me sick
Monday thru Friday
I don't want your "love stick"
Monday thru Friday
I watch these kids
Monday thru Friday
tell me what the hell have you did?
you went to work
you paid the rent
the floor still has dirt
the wall still has that dent
and then you ask where all my time went?
Monday thru Friday
I plan these meals
Monday thru Friday
I make these deals
to pick up these kids
and mop up skidmarks
off the floor
and let these kids
in and out the door
and make their lunches,
planning nutritious food for munchies
and schedule appointments
and put on their ointments

Monday thru Friday
I do all this
and Monday thru Friday
you can't even wash a dish
Monday thru Friday
I'm wiping off sinks
Monday thru Friday
this life stinks
I'm washing clothes
and making sure that their noses
get blown
and buttons get sewn
and matching up socks
and making sure dinners are hot
Monday thru Friday
Monday thru Friday
week after week
day after day
Monday thru Friday
my concentration's blown
Monday thru Friday
I am all alone
thinking of what
needs to be done next
I can't tell my right hand from the left
Monday through Friday
I long for Saturday and Sunday
so that I could get at least one day
of rest
but the weekend is just like its
beginning and its middle
no leisure and no rest
now ain't that some mess?

bathtub

Fuming, we lay side by side,
with stifling lust and leaden anger
lying between us.
Too angry to speak,
too angry to apologize;
we can't make up
not even
to get down.
Angrily, we waste
tender hours,
relentless energy
intense sentiments and
a fantasy not yet conceived.
We could be making a fantasy real,
but we're angry over silly shit.
A silly argument.
You showered and didn't clean
the tub.
I'm wearing a sheer bra and my
nipples are erect and I know you know this.
Your hands aren't on me and
the lights are out, but
still, you know.
You remember and imagine.
And it's so hot.
And just when I think
I have swallowed my anger
and can reach over and
touch you,
it regurgitates
just as fresh as it wants to be

all over again.
And I can't wash it away.
You just don't understand.
I had to clean your dirt
out of the tub.
And I know you regret it.
You regret making me angry.
You wish you could be
making me cum.
If only you had cleaned
the tub…...

nonsense

you keep pulling me back down
you think you're right for me, but
you're wrong
cuz I didn't come from
what you came from, so
really you might not know
any better,
but I do. so what's
my excuse?

your voice

the sound of your voice
irritates me so
much.
I want to talk to you
but can't get past
what you sound like.
if only you could sound
more like how
I want you to sound,
then I'd return your calls.
I have daydreams about
the kinds of conversations
we would have, if only
you didn't sound so
bad.
the drone of your voice
in your messages
just drives me away.
it's so bad I don't listen
to you,
I listen
at you.
and then sometimes
I don't even make it through
your messages.
I just listen long enough
to know its you
and then I press #3
for delete.
I just want to play your
messages back to you,

each and every one
of them,
so you can hear how
awful
you sound.
and each time I listen
to you, I wonder
do you
ever
listen to yourself?
and then I think
that answer must be
no,
because the sound of
your voice is so
horrible,
it must be hard
for even you
to bare
to listen
to.

selfish child

the child who conceals her
pain so you won't worry

shame on you, selfish child

the child who remembers
your birthday and anniversary
because no one else will

shame, shame selfish child

the child who acts as you
expect so you can be proud

selfish, selfish child

the child who can't tell
you how much you hurt
her because she knows
how much it'll hurt you

just as selfish as she can be

what can you do for me?

What can you do for me?
Everything you do, I can do.
Better.
Cook. Clean. Speak. Fix-it-up.
What do you have to offer me?
Love? No.
Security? No.
Lies? Yes.
Adultery? Yes.
Irrationality? Yes.
What can you do for me that I can't do for me?
Pay bills? No.
Make me happy? No.
Fulfill my sexual needs? No.
What on earth can you do for me that I can't do for me?
Disorganization? Yes.
Clutter? Yes.
Confusion? Yes.
Disappointment? Yes.
Why in the hell do I want you?
True love? I don't think so.
Because I pity you? More than likely.
Because I think deep down inside
you want to do the right thing? Probably so.
Because I can envision you
playing with the baby I long to have? Yes.
Well, that's not good enough.
Why do I need to stay here?
Because this is a good life? No.
Because this is a happy marriage? No.
Because we are friends? No.

Because we care about each other? No.
I have stayed because I want to be married,
but not to someone like you.
Because I don't want the stains
and pains and drains and scars of divorce,
though I already have them from marriage?
Because I feel my time for motherhood
is here and will pass me by if I don't grasp it?
Yes.
Yes.
Yes.
Still all not good enough.
What can you do for me that I can't do for myself?
You can make me realize
that my love for me
is more valuable than you.

cry

She tried to cry, but the tears wouldn't come. As she sat sloppily on the floor of the 7-11 reading the center spread about his billion-dollar deal and his life, she really wanted to cry, but she had an extremely hard time squeezing out tears. In a way, she was glad because she knew the tears would sting her bruised cheeks. She had thought of him as she had hurried to this convenience store, as she had limped down the stairs in the parking garage–the parking garage where she had last seen him. Without him, and given this was an even-numbered year, she was alone for the holidays, and she thought of him. She had thought of him lying on the cold concrete, wearing the overcoat she had bought him for his 33rd birthday, sprawled on his back, his head having made a thud that she would never forget as it had hit the concrete. She hoped she would have found him there still, a whole week later, cause of death: gunshot wound to the chest.

She had never heard a gunshot up close and personal. With much trepidation, she had accepted a pistol from a caring friend who had feared for her safety. She had never heard a bullet ever in life, just on TV, and when she had pulled the trigger, she was so startled, so overcome with fear that she'd involuntarily jerked her shoulders and then shook. She had not looked around to see if anyone saw. (Turning to either side would have agitated her whiplashed cervical spine.) She shook all over and then desperately wanted to separate from the thing in her hand that had made the violent, booming noise – another sound she would never forget. She had thrown the gun, her tender clavicle and sternum causing her to grimace (from how he knelt on her chest trying to choke her). She had wanted it out of her hand, out of her sight, away from her battered body, as far away from her as possible, and then, still shaking, she had quickly walked away as fast as her shaking legs and twisted ankle could take her down the stairs of the parking garage.

She had shot him, not during one of his violent moments, but during one of the happiest times of his life. Happy, not with her or their marriage, but because he had been about to close one of the largest investments he'd ever closed. His fledgling business (and his fragile ego) needed the windfall. The day he was scheduled to fly to Atlanta to meet with a wealthy entrepreneur to close the deal, he had been walking away from her, she had been slowly limping behind him (because he'd pushed her causing her to fall and twist her ankle), too angry to touch him, to look in him in the eye, to even hug him a proper farewell, not because they were currently fighting, but because they had fought. He had fought her in such a barbaric, humiliating way, that she couldn't make herself understand why, really, she hadn't left him. She knew his attacks would only worsen with time. And, then there was Paisley. She was glad Paisley had left for the winter break.

He had been walking away from her in the parking garage, a light pep in his step, thrilled that his dreams were finally about to come true, when he had turned around to tell her one last thing. He was walking backward, his lips had formed what turned out to be his last huge, brilliant smile, he had spread his long arms outward, palms facing her as if he were about to perform the largest embrace ever. He had an amazing smile, a million-dollar smile, she had always told him, and a secure and warm embrace. He had taken five steps backward, smiling, arms stretched out wide and had said, "We're billionaires, baby!"

At which point, blank-faced, without a single word, she had pulled the gun from her over coat pocket, pointed it, and shot him with a steadied hand in the upper left chest. All of this had happened, strangely, very smoothly. (Despite her bruised ribs from him having thrown her down the stairs.) She had wondered if she would fumble with the pistol when she had to use it to protect herself. But she didn't fumble or hesitate for one second. It was like the gun had called her sore hand to it with a magnetic force. Her bruised fingers (from fighting him back finally by punching him in the top of his bald head) had locked into place as if they had done this duty a dozen times over. His million-dollar smile had quickly dissolved, and his expression had turned first to a hurt confusion, then to anguish right before the force of the bullet had sent him sprawling backward, feet up in the air, landing headfirst, with his head making that solid, heavy thud and both hands clasped over his chest, legs spread eagle, feet covered in those cheap plastic-looking boots that she had never liked.

Seven days later, she had imagined him still lying there. Thought maybe he was still lying there, maybe needed him to still be lying there, struggling to breathe. Taking heavy exhales with his eyes filled with enormous fear. For a man claiming to be filled with the Holy Spirit (do the faith-filled beat their wives?), who had believed and had recited 1 John 4:4, he had carried entirely too much fear in his heart. This always made her wonder about him. About what secrets he was hiding. Taking the stairs down the parking garage that she had so desperately walked down last week after murdering her husband, as she had passed the second floor, briefly peering out of the stair well hoping to have seen him still lying there on the concrete, the weight of what she had done had come crashing down on her. Her chest hurt. (From where he last punched her between her breasts with ring laden fingers.) Inside, her heart felt like it was being used as a stress ball, firmly and quickly being squeezed, trying to find some sense of normalcy. He had been gone a week, and no one came looking. The anticipation of having to deal with the authorities and his family had been suffocating her. She wondered if anyone knew he was gone. Dead. She had not called the police. Had not filed a missing person's report. She had been too scared to turn on the news or to touch social media. But she had needed to find out if he had been discovered, found. Dead. She had walked with a quicken pace. She had to get to a newspaper to check the obituaries.

Once down the stair well, and out on the busy sidewalk, she couldn't have walked fast enough. Each step on her wrapped ankle had been torture. She had grabbed her purse strap, and grimacing, had pulled it over head and across her chest, clutched it and had begun to slow limp on the sidewalk, heels clicking as she went, looking for the nearest newspaper. Unable to stop herself from the collision, she had bumped chest first into a young woman that had been coming out of the 7-11. "I'm so sorry," she said, wincing. The unapologetic young woman had shoved her back and had shouted, "Murderer!" The shove landed her on the sidewalk, bottom first, outside the convenience store window, exposing her bloodied blouse, and she had scowled as she had used her fractured elbow (from when he twisted her arm as she tried to get away) to break her fall. Slowly rolling over and painfully pulling herself up, she had seen a stack of newspapers inside by the storefront window.

She had entered the convenience store, grabbed a newspaper, knelt, and began frantically turning the pages. Was I a murderer? She had thought. (His post-mortem mind games still trying to confuse her.) Her fingerprints had been on the gun. It would be found, and she would go to prison. How would she face his family? Had seven days really passed? Turning the newspaper pages one by one, she had scanned the whole newspaper. She toppled over, slumped with her bandaged forehead (from where he had banged her head into the wall) in the center of the paper. She had not seen his obituary, or a double-paged spread covering his murder in the newspaper. In disbelief, she sat up, closed the newspaper, and flipped it over, where she had seen his picture printed on the back page, his million-dollar smile right there, with his name and billion-dollar deal headlined in bold black Times New Roman font at the top center of the page, a continuation from the business section.

Moaning aloud and gently bumping her bandaged, numb forehead onto the newspaper that was on the less than clean store floor, desperately needing to cry, she could not. So, she read the article, on the floor in the 7-11, looking for a clue as to whether she was really the murderer the passerby accused her of being (his narcissism made her question her entire existence). There were no tears to express the agony she felt. She undoubtedly loved him, but her pain was not because she missed him; this sorrow was because he had made her become like what she most despised about him: violent.

❀ ❀

She squeezed her eyes tightly wanting desperately to release the pain that resided in her gut, (from where he kicked her with those cheap boots), but she could not. "What have I done?" She thought. She sniffled, uncontrollably, but no tears came.

"What have I done?" she mumbled quietly, repeatedly, with eyes tightly shut. She felt sweat trickle down her temple, and she stopped sniffling. She turned her head left, then right, hearing the rustle of the fabric stuck to her matted and damp hair, her cervical spine now throbbing.

"What am I going to do?" she muttered. A long exhale brought her fully awake. Disgusted her with the damp satin pillow brushing against the back of her bruised neck, she turned left again to face the doorway, (and grimaced from her ripped earlobe, the result of him reaching to pull her ponytail and getting his fingers caught in her hoop earrings) the direction from which another long exhale unsettled her. She opened her eyes, and the pitch black filled them (or at least the left one because the right one was still swollen, nearly shut from him having punched it). She stared into the darkness trying to focus on her daughter's face, hoping it would center her and bring about some light. She blinked a few times, trying to reorient herself and dared not look to the right side of the bed. Without turning her head, left eye wide open, yet seeing nothing, she slid her trembling hand between the sheets to the right side of the bed to make certain he was not there. He wasn't. Just the sink hole he left in the too-soft mattress remained. She heard another heavy breath and sat up, the gun that rested on her belly while she slept slid into her satin covered lap.

"Paisley?" she whispered into the shadows emerging before her. "Paisley!" She couldn't remember whether Paisley was home or not. (Constant fear of him clouded her memory.)

Not a sound from her daughter. She gripped the silencer-tipped pistol.

"Over here, love," he said. Looking toward the window seat, the darkness gave way to a large shadow seated next to the slender Christmas tree. Squinting her eyes, wiping sweaty bangs from her brows with the back of her hand (that had the stitches she'd gotten when he sliced her with the razor, she'd used in defense against him), she placed her finger on the trigger, her brain fog dissipating. How'd he get here? She thought.

"We're going to be billion—"

With a quick aim and green laser guidance, she pointed the gun toward his broad torso, raised it to aim at his shadowy head. She fired. She saw long limbs limp sprawl onto the seat cushion. No, not "we"—just me, she thought as she laid back down in her bed.

She tried to cry but the tears wouldn't come.

"Mommy?!"

pitiful man

pitiful man
need a woman to hold your hand
you can't stand
on your own
you'd rather move into her home
with her mother
and still have some other
chic on the side
and then wonder why
your life is so fucked up
pitiful man
I can't stand
you
make me sick
trying to lure me in with your dick
into your drama
come crying to me like I'm your mama
that's why your life is so fucked up
pitiful man
you think I'm like other ladies
to let you make me a baby
just so I can keep you
you asshole, I already knew
what you were about
talking bout how you bout to lose your house
and how your car AC just went out
trying to get me to give you money
like all yo other dumbass honey's
that's why your life is so fucked up
pitiful man
trying to help me solve my problems

when we both know you don't care to solve em
all your screw-ups you blame on your papa
and you know damn well he didn't cause your drama
c'mon, grow up, come to grips
I have and I put my hand on my hips
I'm not taking one step further
and that wife of yours, you better act like you heard her
when she said it's her life too that you so fucked up
pitiful man
from now on I won't listen to your lies
right now I'm saying bye-bye
when I've said my peace I'm gonna leave
yes sir, yeah buddy, you'd better believe
but before I go, I'll give you this
yeah, I do love your lips
and yeah, I think you are attractive
but to keep me captive
no, that just ain't enough
cause you still a pitiful man
and my life you won't fuck up.

yo-yo

you shove me out the door
then you let me back in
no, no
I'm not your yo-yo
you knock me down
then reach me your hand to get back up
no, no,
I'm not your yo-yo
you dress me up so elegantly
then strip me down to shreds
no, no
I'm not your yo-yo
you water me
and then you suck me dry
no, no
I'm not your yo-yo

be

if I could just be
who I want to be
then you would
really see me
for who I am
and who I could
be but somehow
you keep me from
being me knowing
me trusting me and
so I remain content
being who you need
me to be what a sad
way to be.

beautiful man

we're just fooling ourselves to
think we're right for each other
and something meaningful
will come from this cuz I have
a beautiful man that I will
never let go of, not that you're
not beautiful. you do have beautiful ways
but you are someone else's beautiful
man. and not mine. not mine. you are
not mine. and you never will be
because you never could be.
for starters, you don't know how.

the lesson here

Is this thing with you really about me?
Are your indiscretions really about me?
And how after all this time I don't really know how to love you?
To show affection for you?
Maybe your infidelities are the result of me,
But I am not the cause. The cause is you.
In a commitment, you also commit to find a resolution within.
What is my lesson here?
And do I have to remain here to learn it and live it?
Can I learn my lesson and move on to live it anew?

less is more

less is more;
more or less.
the more I say,
the less you hear;
the less you say,
the more I want you;
the more I complain,
the less you give;
the less you give,
the more I complain;
the less I want you,
the more you give;
the more you give,
the more I want you;
the more you take
the less I have;
the less I have,
the more I need you;
more is less;
more or less,
give or take.

let's be real

She looks at the very first picture they took
together and thinks "who were we"?
Who were those people?
He was a newly separated military man
She was a semi-naïve college girl full of hope.
He was refreshing, slightly older, big, strong,
he seemed mature and secure.
And honest
enough to tell her he had a son
and he would tell her sweet things.
that she was sexy and that he loved her
And she would believe him.
And he would cook for her,
Make sure his apartment was so clean
for her,
He would draw her bath water and
bathe her.
He would undress her after she'd fallen asleep in her clothes
They would go for walks, for jogs.
But the reality is that he was still married and he
was not honest, not
completely.
And he was seeing someone else
and he always had been.
Has there ever been a time
when he was only seeing one person?
The reality is that when she would visit him
they would stay locked up in his apartment
sexed up. Holed up, shut in.
And they would be shut in.
And no one would come over.

And they wouldn't take visitors.
all because he was seeing someone else?
And then they traveled across country
and he asked her to marry him
with this little bitty ring
that didn't even fit her finger.
Symbolism.
And the ring didn't matter anyway
because he couldn't marry her
and he knew it.
Because he was still married to another.
And then God gave her a life.
And then he went overseas.
And he swore by phone,
overseas how much he loved her.
And she, then scared
and confused and
wanting something,
Someone better for herself,
she let that life go.
Smart.
The reality is that he
was seeing
someone else over there.
But then she didn't care
because she had lost weight.
And she was beautiful,
and wanted and dating and
having seeing others, too.
So now what?
And then she left him
because she'd had enough.
And then she went back to him
because of tragedy.

And then they decided to marry.
Because of tragedy?
And then he went overseas again,
and she planned their entire wedding,
their entire initial life together
without much help from him because
he was too involved
over there with other women,
other things.
Yet all the while
professing his love
and commitment to her.
And that wasn't ok.
The reality is that then she was true.
She was for real. She was committed
And then they got married.
and everything remained wrong.

compelling

it's compelling that after
all you've done to me
I'm still standing
triumphantly
you could not beat me
I wobbled but,
my spirit keeps me free—you
couldn't take that away from me

stronger than me

I need somebody
Stronger than me to challenge
me when I'm not me.

get up

I need to get up from
here wipe away these
tears bitchslap my
fear swallow my
pride why should I
hide the way I
feel it's gonna
kill me to keep on like
this without a
kiss a care a touch
I miss so much
company close to me
fear and shame entrap me—
get up off of me so I can
get up!

eight

"I love to be alone. I never found a companion that was so
companionable as solitude."

— HENRY DAVID THOREAU

silence of solitude

heart's conversation
with the mind, inaudible
deep, continuous

sad song

This song makes me sad
Makes me remember things
I tried to forget.

time off

Time off allows me to slow down and think. Sometimes life gets us going so fast that we're just moving on auto pilot. Yesterday, I heard several ideas on varying topics that gave me pause. Time off allows me to slow down, steer my own ship, and process a few quotes on monitoring one's thinking, faith, hypocrisy, leadership, and opposition.

"Don't believe everything you think." Essentially, this means make sure your thoughts, opinions, whatever, are based on fact, otherwise, those false thoughts and beliefs can lead you to disastrous actions.

"Don't let a hypocrite lead you to hell." Basically, no one is perfect. There is only one perfect being. We all fall short—even those people that we most respect, be them parents, world leaders, religious leaders, what have you. Don't let the shortcomings of people cause you to lose your faith or become discouraged. Instead, because we are human, expect that we will make mistakes, but also expect that people deal with the mistakes appropriately—confessing them, apologizing for them, accepting responsibility, and trying not to repeat them.

"Look past the leader." Our leaders make mistakes. Our leaders are human. Our leaders will not always succeed with everything they attempt to do. Be happy that they had the courage to try. And, if our leaders are willfully doing bad things, willfully leading others in the wrong direction, be confident in knowing that there is One who will hold those leaders accountable. So, instead of losing your faith or getting all twisted up over those who refuse to do the right thing, have comfort in knowing that all things happen for a reason and eventually, all wrongs will be made right. Have faith in the One who leads the leader, as opposed to the leader himself.

Additionally, when something good and divine begins to happen, there will be "haters," simply put. Not everyone likes change. Not everyone will want to have positive improvement. Some are more comfortable with the status quo. Many will not understand why it's necessary to change or improve. If you've ever felt hated on because you were trying to do something good, something different, something better, just know that this is normal.

Lastly, life is full of opposition. We have to expect that there will be opposition. Opposition is **not** a reason to quit. It is **not** a sign that we're doing the wrong thing, but rather just the opposite. Perhaps it's a sign that we're doing the right thing because whenever there's someone bold enough to say what many want to say or do what others want to do, rest assured there will be haters. Sometimes opposition is a sign that we are getting that much closer to our goal so, persist despite whatever obstacles come your way.

I was really blessed to have had time to reflect on those messages. We don't always have the time to reflect but reflection is critical to growth.

life's expediency

Life goes by too fast. Often, I think, "when I'm gone, who will remember me and what will they say?" More importantly, what will my daughter say, and how she will remember me and what would she do without me? Because I understand the pain of losing a parent or wishing a parent were here, I don't want her to experience that pain. As parents, we want to shield our children from pain and bare it for them, but there's no real way we can.

Today is Friday the 13th, and I don't believe in that stuff, but today nothing at all went the way I planned it. I had planned to drop her off early to day camp, go do my grocery shopping, see one or two movies, come home color my hair, do some online shopping, read my bible then get my hair cut and either read my bible more or rent a movie. (Very exciting, I know). Very little of that went as planned. I was, however, able to treat myself to a nice lunch—sushi salmon, snapper, yellow tail, salmon skin, seaweed—it was awesome! I thanked God for a tasty and quiet lunch.

I'd been running all day and when I finally got home and showered, I sat down and just started bawling from the stress of just going, and going, and going and thinking, and thinking and thinking. One of the major downsides of single parenthood is that there isn't someone to share the thinking of what's best for the family. No shared responsibility of those decisions or failures. I was tired of thinking of what to do, what to buy, how to stretch my money, how not to disappoint my daughter. And so, I bawled.

Then I pulled out the TV from the utility room. I gave up watching TV almost a year ago because I realized it was a source of stress. TV made me ignore my daughter, made me shoo her away because I had to listen to something else. TV was a distraction from the real issues in my life. TV was cluttering my head, and I had too many other things to think about. I had to be home by a certain hour to watch something on TV. (I didn't have cable – gave that up about four years ago. No TiVO). TV helped to make me anxious. And I realized the same was true for my daughter. When she was watching TV, and I needed to talk to her, her mood changed drastically. She'd have tantrums. The impact was strong.

When my mom visited, she brought her little TV for my daughter, and she left it here with me. I think she felt badly that I didn't have one, thought maybe I missed it. But really, I "gave it up" because my TVs broke. Both of them. At once. Talk about signs. During the time I spent with broken TVs, I realized what a bad affect they were having on my daughter and I and so, I chose not to buy another one. Chose to live my life instead of watching others live theirs.

So, I put the TV away, in the utility room, when my mom left. But tonight—having some down time and not having rented that movie I wanted to rent—I pulled out the TV because I remembered seeing that there'd be a movie on broadcast network TV tonight. I turned it on and saw two things that moved me to more tears.

I caught the end of a Dateline show on a teacher, whom I'm assuming is first year and about how she pushed her students and about how, at first, they were failing, but passed with Bs in the end, and how the kids were dealing with tough family situations, and how she wouldn't let up or give up on them and how she realized in the end, how inadequate she was and all that she still needed to learn, but also how much she had accomplished, that she met her goal, that she did impact her students positively. This teacher's story touched me. I saw a caring teacher who seemed like she had found her calling. And I was proud of this lady, though I'd never met her. And I share with her, this stranger, the weight of what it means to be a teacher. And I thought of my own successes and my own shortcomings. And I was very moved.

As Dateline was going off, and I was pulling myself together, I then saw a preview for a special on the death of Tim Russert. I didn't even know he'd passed away! I'd watch his show on Sunday mornings as I would get ready for church. He seemed really real, really personable, really smart, lots of integrity. He was funny and he seemed humble. Then I heard them say heart attack, died at work, 58 and then I thought: he never even knew that his last day was actually going to be his last day.

That's the scariest thing of all, I think. And then, I bawled more. Not just because of my stressful day that was supposed to be stress free, but because of all the things I focused on today – all the wrong things. And I thought, what if today were my last day? Did I focus on the important things? I only spent the morning with my daughter; she spent the day and will spend the night with her granny. It was just me busying myself around the city, driving in the hot sun, watching the gas gauge needle going down, down, down, as I'm driving in the hot sun, burning up dollars of gas, busying myself with errands that don't matter much. Things going around and around in my head that don't matter much. I thought: is this the way I'd want to spend my last day?

Then, I thought of Russert's cause of death—heart attack. I know that I've not lived as healthily as I could have thus far, exercising one season out of the year, stressing too much, not getting enough sleep, and I wonder what kind of damage I've already done to my body, my heart.

Russert was a dad and his own dad outlived him. And with Father's Day this weekend, I began to think for the first time in a little while about my own dad. Usually when this holiday comes I around, I make sure I'm pretty numb. Not from substance abuse or anything like that, but by compartmentalizing. I lost my dad 11 years ago in May. And I miss him so much. I lost him when I was 24 and, in my opinion, when I was just becoming an adult. And I just wonder what advice he'd have to give me about all these things I was running around, stressing myself out over. I wish he were here to enjoy his beautiful grandchildren.

Even after 11 years, there's a certain part of me, a little piece of me that still hasn't processed that he's really not here. My mom is still here, and I pray she knows how much I love her—life would be really different without her. However, life has been really different now for 11 years. Moms and dads are equally important, just in very different ways. So today, I'm putting a picture of my dad on social media in remembrance of him, wishing he could feel how much he's missed and still loved.

And, tonight I realized that all this "running around," not just today but over the last two months, has gotten me out of step with the will of God. And I felt like an idiot because I was able to get so distracted, so easily. And I had to stop and ask for forgiveness and ask God to guide me because he's blessed me with a beautiful little someone that I have to guide.

And she just turned five…that's where the "life goes by too fast" part comes in. She's so smart. If you've never thought a five-year-old could make you feel like an idiot, just wait until you have a five-year-old. I wonder when she got so smart and so tall. She's always been beautiful, but right now she's more than half my height and so smart. Like a sponge. She's watching everything I do and listening to everything I say and everything everyone else says. This morning—and this might gross some of you out—I was putting on her bathing suit, which meant panties had to come off. And when the panties came off, there were little folded up pieces of tissue paper in them.

I asked her why she did that and she said because "I saw you put those 'things' in yours." And, I'll leave it at that. If you get it, you get it, if not, it wasn't meant for you. At any rate, she notices and remembers everything.

I'm 34 years old and right now I'm wishing the years would slow down. A small part of me is fearful that once it's all done, I will not have done what I was put here to do. And I am really not too far off from the age my dad was when he died. I guess, I'm feeling my own mortality. And I'm looking at all this gray hair in my head and wondering when on Earth did it pop up?

I just want what I do while I'm here to matter. So tonight, that's my prayer.

i stand still

I stand still
when I'm not moving
and I'm not doing
what I should be doing so,
I stand still. Yet,
my mind is always
moving,
thinking of what I
should be doing. Yet
I stand still.
Overwhelmed
by the thought of
choosing a direction
in which to move so, justly
I stand still.

i am listening

I am listening
to the circular rattle of air
touching my skin as I lay I am
listening to a Broadway-like tune with orchestra
sounds that make my eardrums sore I am
listening to an imaginary ring as I stare at the phone
longing to pick it up I am
listening to pedicured balls of feet
rub against each other restlessly I am
listening to frayed hair sifting through fingers
that desire to probe something new I am
listening to a palm turned sideways slide to
the beginning at the end of each line I am
listening to fingertips tickle
a navel encircled by fine black hairs I am
listening to the rustle of a shirttail
tugged out of a loss of words I am
listening to air slowly dragged into
lungs and smoothly blown out as breath I am
listening to the flicking of a soft brittle
nail against a tooth I am
listening to the rhythmic whine of a deep
voice begging forgiveness I am
listening to waves
skip over me I am
listening to sand
squish between my toes I am
listening to rocks ricochet
across glistening water I am
listening to blue sunshine
sing my name I am

listening to white drops
stain my shirt as I run I am
listening to finely crushed
pink ice trickle down my throat I am
listening to trees
laughing together I am
listening to fruit
split wide open I am
listening to the silence
of thoughts I am
listening to a wish
for inspiration
I am
listening.

nine

"A mother understands what a child does not say."

—A JEWISH PROVERB

silence of a mother's heart

a mother's heart holds
countless treasures unspoken,
things enigmatic.

where do pork chops come from?

We were eating fried porkchops covered with bran cereal, which was quite tasty, by the way, and she asked, "Do porkchops swim?"

I laughed and said, "No."

She said, "Where do they come from?"

"Porkchops come from pigs."

"Do pigs like to eat porkchops?"

I laughed again and said, "No."

"What do they eat?"

"They eat lots of stuff."

"But where do porkchops come from?" she asked again, unwilling to accept my first response.

So, I finally said, "Remember earlier today when we bought them from Wal-Mart? Porkchops come from Wal-Mart."

And then she was satisfied and kept right on eating.

tutu cute

Bella dancerealla tutu on her,
i found a scarf and said,
"let me make you a dress."
my handmade dress slipping
off her shoulder, frustrated her,
so, i pinned it.
she put on heeled dress-up shoes;
i put a scarf around her neck,
my chain belt around her tiny waist.
i brushed my makeup on her
little babysoft cheeked canvass.
she looked in the mirror
on my sliding mirror closet door,
edges of her painted lips
beginning to curl.
delighted at the sight
of herself
with my lipstick on,
she smiled at herself
and then at me.

save the rest

I made coffee,
and with tears in my eyes,
I sat on the side of my bed. I was so
        Overwhelmed
        that I had to sit down and pray
for guidance
on what needed to be done today.
        I was guided to play with my daughter and wash clothes.
And write.
        Then, while still morning, precisely 8:45AM,
        my girlfriend called.
        She asked me if I was sleeping.
"No, I was so
        overwhelmed,
        I had to sit down
        and pray for guidance."
        "You know, you're going through
                a lot right now," she said.
                "And, you're
                        too hard on yourself.
                        Mothers try
        to do so much
                in a day and really, we—just
                can't
                do
                it
                all. What we have to do is
                choose
        one to three things to do,
                focus
        on those and save
        the rest for another day."

Love of Nature

Written and Directed by "Kammie Yammie Pie"

Starring:

Fish
Bird
Cat
Elephant
Koala Bear
Dog
Horse

Act One

Elephant: Hi Cat.
Dog: Cat, Bird is coming to visit.
Horse: I am happy to hear that. Bird makes the sweetest sounds.
Cat: Where is she going to stay?
Koala Bear: In a nest.
Fish: Yes, everyone knows that.
All: Yes! Let's have a party!

THE END.

tattler

I opened the door. He was standing there in wrinkled jeans, black shoes, stripped shirt. He looked pathetic. Or, his clothes did, because I never looked him in the face. It hurt too much, and anger prevented me from doing so. So, instead, I chose to look at his shoes. She walked out the door with the book she was reading in her hand.

"I'll see you in a little while," I said.

"Bye mommy."

Then they started down the stairs. Her first, with her book in hand and then him, carrying the boxes I had just emptied, cautiously placing his feet on the steps so he wouldn't trip.

She was only three steps down, and she was already telling him about our day.

"Daddy, you know what?" she said. "My mommy put some make up on me and then she dressed me up and put on a belt and then I put some "lipglops" on mommy, and then we danced and listened to the radio."

As I shut the door, I thought to myself if I ever did begin to date again, her dad would be the first to know. Everything we do, she tells him about it. Innocently, but still.

dipped in the water

We were watching a John Legend video on my computer and there were three backup singers—two ladies and a guy. One lady had on a short, slim dress with naturally curly hair and large, pretty earrings. The camera flashed on this particular backup singer and my kiddo said, "I like that lady, mama."

It flashed so quickly I didn't notice which one she was talking about. The camera showed her again, and again she said, "Mama, I like that lady." And then I saw her before the camera flashed away.

"What do you like about her?" I asked.

She said, "I like her earrings."

When I saw her again to study the lady's earrings, I said, "Those are cute earrings."

Then she was quiet. I knew she was thinking about something else. Finally, she said, "I want her to be my mommy."

That went right to my heart.

"Why do you want her to be your mommy?"

She said, "She's a cute little lady."

"Oh." Processing, I asked her, "Well, what if I said I wanted a new daughter?"

She giggled and at first, she said through her laugh, "Noooo!"

So, I repeated my question to her hoping she'd answer, and she did.

"You could have one,' she said.

I asked her, "How?"

She said, "If you dip me in the water, you could have a new daughter."

And that was the end of that.

Speechless.

Profound.

God.

standing next to Jesus

She was sitting on the floor taking the barrettes out of the box and putting them into the bags. I had just shown her a picture of me, a cousin, and a friend when we were in high school, and she asked, "Where was I mommy?"

And I said, "Well, you weren't born yet. God hadn't made you yet."

She continued putting barrettes into the bag and said, "Yeah, I was with God. Standing next to Jesus."

I looked at her, and she was still putting the barrettes in the bag. She wasn't looking at me and had not even stopped to look at me.

She said, "Remember, mommy? I was standing next to Jesus, and then you called me home. Remember?"

I was amazed. I stopped right in the middle of putting another shirt on a hanger, dropped them both on the bed and just stared at her. She seemed so serious. She never looked at me to get my reaction. She kept contently putting the barrettes away.

I was so amazed. I smiled, and all I could say was, "Yes," in agreement.

She repeated, "Yeah, I was standing next to God, then you called me home."

And she said this as though she had a clear memory of standing next to Jesus himself. It was like she thought something was wrong with me because I couldn't remember.

My thought trail landed me at my labor experience and how after, 29 hours of labor, I had a C-section because she and I both had fever, her head was turned upside down, and after she emerged from my birth canal, it was realized that she had swallowed some amniotic fluid which had her first bowel movement it, thus she had difficulty breathing and went up to NICU for seven days. (I was hospitalized, too. For six days due to a uterine infection acquired during the long labor.)

And I wonder if my prayers for her birth—for her life—were answered and, rather than taking her life, God sent her back to be born to me alive to love and raise?

It fills my heart that she knows the comfort of standing next to Jesus. She was in the safest place I know.

let the little children come to me - matthew 19:14

I got in bed with her, thinking this would be a change for her. Usually, she hops in bed with me to wake me up. She giggled, happy to have me lying beside her. Last night before we went to bed, we said our prayers together, but she didn't remember.

"Mommy, did you say your prayers?"

"Yes, I said mine with you," I said.

"Well, you didn't ask for forgiveness for the Holy Ghost," she said, taunting me.

She caught me off guard, and I just looked at her, thinking surely my four-year old child isn't judging me. It was as if she knew of something I'd done wrong and that she wanted me to repent.

"What do you mean by that?" I asked her.

"There's power in the Holy Spirit," she said.

"There sure is," I told her.

ten

"Come into the silence of solitude, and the vibration there will talk to you through the voice of God."

— PARAMAHANSA YOGANANDA

silence of my soul

in the soul silence
one is able to discern
God's luminous voice.

whole

there are moments when I am ashamed
of the pieces of me.
not the whole,
but the pieces—the pieces of me
that were used improperly,
impulsively, unwisely,
indiscretionally,
improperly.
there are pieces that I wish would fall off
completely.
but these pieces, they make up me.
they belong to me
define me
compose me.
i am them, and they are me
indefinitely.
however, God has already forgiven me
for those little pieces that shame me
and i don't want to shame Thee
by continually feeling shamefully
about these little pieces that define those parts of me;
for the definition of your forgiveness is to believe and be set free
and therefore, i am not defined by me but by Thee and
in Thee
and for that i have no shame. thank you, Lord,
for reminding me daily
that, in you, i can live wholly
all because i surrendered my everything to Thee.
thank you for allowing your body to hang brokenly
so that, in you, mine could have a new shame-free assembly.
thank you, Lord, for wholly loving me—
every little broken piece.

gospel

I look at the gospel
singers and wonder why
they don't cry while
they sing the songs
that make me cry.
is it God?

lately

I don't know what's wrong with me these days.
These days, it's hard to do what I said I'd do.
These days, what's most important is on the backburner,
and some other stuff has floated to the top.
These days, I have more questions than answers.
These days, I can't remember what I need to remember.
These days, keep going faster and faster—
they have no beginning and no end.
These days, I look at her and wonder who she'll be.
These days, I look at her and can't believe I'm her mommy.
These days, I'll soon wish I could redo.
These days, dear Lord, I give to You.
I pray these days that You order my steps.
I pray these days that Your will be done.
I pray these days that You use me, dear Lord.
I pray that these days are filled with love.
These days dear Lord, I've grown closer to You.
These days help me do what You want me to do.
I pray that these days glorify You.

finding God in Nemo

Part of my prayer early on was that I want him to be happy, largely so that as I'm finding my happiness, he'll be able to let go of me and won't be looking at me crazy. But I didn't mean for him to move on now. So, when I saw those pictures the day I stopped by to get some of my things, I wasn't completely surprised because I know how he operates. But I'd be lying if I didn't say that my heart stopped. I was ready to leave the house; yet something was calling me to that bedroom to look for the shirt I'd come there for. Something was calling me to look in the closet for it. I went in there, and it was full of his shirts. Not mine. So, I turned around ready to leave, but noticed the TV working that he said didn't work and the pictures beside the TV. Of another woman. In a thong and a bra. Two like that: one where you could see her rear and the other with her leaned forward hands on her knees with her belly hanging down on her thighs. There was one more of her and her daughter. And there was a card beneath all three pictures. My young daughter was standing there beside me, and I didn't want her to see these pictures; yet I needed to read that card. So, I snatched up all of it—the three pictures and the card and stuffed them in my back jeans pocket, pulling my shirt down over it all. And then all I wanted to do was leave as quickly as I could. Partly because I didn't know if he was on his way home. The other part was because I needed to be as far away from him as possible and being in the house where he now lives alone was way too close to him.

When I got home that evening, all I could do was think about that picture. On the inside, I was sad—stunned might be a better word choice. So much so that I couldn't cry. I felt let down, in a sense. Even though *I* decided to leave. Even though *I* decided I didn't want *him*. I felt like a weight was on my chest. Yet, I couldn't express any of this. My daughter was watching me. It's scary sometimes how much attention little kids pay to adults. I didn't want her to see me crying.

My daughter and I drove home in the dark, and for the most part, it was quiet. I think that even though she didn't know what had just occurred, what I had just found, and even though I did my best to disguise what I was feeling, I think that she knew I was sad. Usually, she talks and talks and talks. This time she didn't. I didn't turn on the music. I just wanted silence. And she let me have it, for most of the way. For the other part of the way, she sang. She sang soft, impromptu songs about Jesus, which I really appreciated. She was on a quiet roll, and I was amazed. When you expose your children to Jesus, teach them about Jesus, the ways in which they can, in turn, bless you, is awesome. She does this often, and it seems her songs, be them made up or real, are sung always at the right time.

So, at home I knew I wanted to read that card and look at this woman one more time. I was anxious about it, but I played it really cool. I took my time in getting her ready for bed. Maybe too much time. I was trying hard to make her think everything was fine, but I think, in trying really hard, maybe she thought I was just being weird. Finally, I got her to sleep and pulled out those pictures from my purse. I read the card. Looked at the pictures of the woman in her lingerie and her and her daughter. All I could think about was what on Earth he told her to get next to her. My best girlfriend says that there are always woman out there waiting for a man. This woman looks too happy. I just wonder if she realizes what she's getting. Not knowing what to do with the pictures, I put them back in my purse. I was tired of taking filth from that house and bringing it here. I already have a boxful full of his pornography in the hatch of my SUV. And two pornographic DVDs in the front of my car. Now that I think about it, whenever I go get my car serviced, if there are nosey service guys, and they dig too deep, they might be looking at me strangely because of that crap in my car.

At any rate, I got my bible from the bathroom, and all I could do was pray. I still couldn't cry. Each time before I begin reading my bible, I pray for understanding and clarity and for a word that will help me through. It was when I bowed my head to pray that finally I cried. I've been trying hard to be real with God and in doing so, I tell him what's really in my heart. My mind wasn't allowing me to feel hurt over those pictures. But when I pray, I pray with my heart, and my heart was hurt. When I confessed it to God, I cried. Then I called my best girlfriend and told her about it (which I probably should've just left it with God). Surprisingly, I didn't feel better after I talked to her about it. I just felt like I was snitching on somebody. And then two days later when my mom called, I told her a brief version, and now I'm over it.

✿ ✿

Last week I bought a kite that was a colorful fish, perhaps inspired by *Finding Nemo*. During the whole week I watched "Finding Nemo" about seven times and *Hitch* about five. Something about these movies captivated me. *Finding Nemo* was mostly a humorous adventure, with touching moments, and I was able to connect with the animated characters. *Hitch* was humorous, insightful, relatable.

There was a line in *Finding Nemo* that struck me. The line was from the scene when Dori and Marlin were inside the whale, and they were holding on to the whale's tongue trying not to fall down his throat. Dori, assured that everything would be alright, wanted to let go of the whale's tongue and fall into its throat. Marlin, unsure, didn't want to let go because he thought they'd just be eaten. The whale "spoke" to Dori, and because she "speaks "whale," when Marlin asked what the whale said, she translated the whale's call to, "It's time to let go." That line struck me. When Marlin asked, "How do you know everything will be okay?" Dori said, "I don't."

That's faith. Right there. That's simple faith—trusting when you don't know how it'll turn out, yet having a sense that it will be fine. While they were talking about taking their fins off the whale's tongue and trusting that they'd be alright, perhaps Marlin was also realizing that he needed to stop worrying so much and perhaps loosen the reigns off his son, Nemo. However, that line made me consider what things of which I needed to let go. Like my marriage. After finding those pictures, it seems that I was the only one still holding on. That it's time to stop looking backward at it and start looking ahead. And with that, I decided to sell my wedding rings and let that be the end. My daughter can see them in pictures. If she wants.

receiving gifts

Opening the door, I glanced at the presents under the tree, sort of making sure they were still there, put my jacket on the arm of the couch because there's no coat hanger or coat closet, took off my backpack, walked across the living room to put my keys on the bar. I looked at the table to find her half-eaten breakfast—the one I worked so quickly to fix from scratch when I didn't really have the time—still sitting on the table. Barely touched. Biscuit with just one bite, scrambled eggs picked over. When I say from scratch, what I mean is actually cooked on the stove. The days go by so fast now that usually my cooking is done in the microwave—rice, vegetables— anything I can microwave, you'd better believe I will.

I walked through the kitchen to see dishes in the sink, foil-wrapped biscuits, and I stopped in the doorway to peer into her room. Sunlight shining through the blinds that still have no curtains up after six months. The sunlight drew me in and so, I walked down to her room to find it's a mess. No other way to say it. Just a plain mess. But before I could even get to complaining good about just how messy it is, I saw four little baby dolls, each with blankets over them. One of them was in front of the bathroom door. Another by the utility room. And two in her doorway. Then, I remembered her playing with her dolls this morning before we left. She was sitting in her doorway, patting them and talking to them, just as her teachers talked to her and her school friends. This is one of her favorite things to do. She was all dressed for school, all ready to go. Just waiting for me, as usual. And, as I was putting on my shirt in my room, I peered from my bedroom, down the hallway to find her sitting and patting those babies. And so, looking at those babies laying there now made me smile. That's the beauty of little kids. You can't wait to get a break and the minute you realize you have a break, you yearn for them to be back. Instantly, I missed her and wondered what she was getting into at school.

I went into my room, clothes on top of the treadmill. Apparently, it's hard for me to hang up clothes, and I'll use whatever furniture possible as hangers—door edges, drawers pulled out slightly. I pulled my sheets off my bed, oh, about three weeks ago and still haven't washed them. Our winter is trying to come on in and those satin sheets are no good in winter. Knowing this, I haven't been motivated to get them washed and back on the bed. They won't keep me warm anyhow. My room (and all other rooms) is also void of curtains. I was adamant about taking the curtains and rods from the house and have yet to hang them. Too much work, and I don't want to end up with holes in the walls and no curtains up. They are somewhat folded in the utility room, just waiting for me to reveal them again.

As I sat on my bed, trying to purge the filthy images I've just seen (from a bad movie, not speaking of my untidy house) from my mind, I realize that the shower is dripping. I noticed it when I got up at 2:30 this morning, but my morning went by so fast that I forgot to fix that. And so now, its late afternoon, and still, it drips. And it's quiet. Almost too quiet. I put on the air conditioner because, as our winter tries to come in, we still have some high 70, even 80-degree days. Today was one of them. It's been a while since I've had to use it, and now it smells a little mildewy.

But it's quiet. It's been four and a half years since I've been able to just think of me. Have my own space, without a "Mama….", "Mama…", "Mama…" I'm reminded of my single days. But I can't stay there too long. Those were confusing days. But, as I sit here, I am thankful. Thankful to have my own space, even if I don't really own it. My own space. Just me and her. Sometimes I pretend like I'm in a movie, you know the ones when the actors come home to their little studio apartment. I love the ones that look like old warehouses. I bet they'd be cool to live in. Spacious. No yucky carpet. High ceilings. Until then, I'm content with what I have, although getting a little crowded with the stuff I keep bringing over from the house, little pieces of that other life. I'm content that my life is *my* life now—free from so much of that emotional mess so that I can listen and hear and do what I am supposed to do. Dr. Robert Neville did it and he's not even real. I know I can.

Sitting in the quiet, I began to reflect on last night. It was an awesome night. Maybe not to most, but it was for me. Looking at her babies and the presents reminded me of it. She and I had just finished getting ready for bed, our showers were done, and we had eaten. I'd made tuna. It went quite smoothly. No tantrums. I'd fussed at her a little on the way home because she pinched a friend at school. She was sitting at the dinner table watching Dora on DVD, as I was preparing to work my second job, when the doorbell rang. It was them. I really don't know what to call them. I'll go with "a blessing."

They'd helped us during the summer pay our rent and our utility bill, and they called about two weeks ago to ask if we needed something else. When I first got their message, I didn't call back. I'd sent them the thank-you card for their help during the summer that pride and speechlessness kept me from sending right away. But I did it. I sent one to all who helped me…all but one that I forgot when it fell on the floor in the foyer the day, I went to the post office. I promised myself that I would send it.

It had been a very humbling summer. An ascent, I've been calling it, and I have a mountain as my screen saver to remind me of it. It reminded me of being in Colorado. Something about seeing all those mountains, all that nature all at one time helped me to know that there is something much, much bigger than me at work here. At that time, I'd felt closer to God than I'd felt in a long time. Being there and then being in Hawaii last year and looking at all that ocean. I couldn't explain it. I've had lots of family die, watched my dad die (one of those confusing times), got married, even went through labor (though, I was drugged for most of that). Something about being where I was at that time allowed me a deeper understanding of God.

I even sent a thank-you to mom, a thank-you I know she didn't need because she's always there to help. I wanted to let her know, though, that it meant a lot because she's single now and has her own set of needs. I don't think there's ever been a time when she's said she can't help. We expect family to help and usually take them for granted. But when a stranger step in—that's awesome. This couple didn't know me. They don't know that my child is actually mine. They didn't know that I won't go and sell off these gifts. But I'm hoping that they've seen my heart and intentions through God's eyes and that they had a sense of me via Him.

So, this couple, the ones that had been a blessing during the summer called me about two weeks ago to ask if we needed anything for Christmas. They informed that they do a wish-tree for families that they'd helped before, and they had thought of us. And I'm so glad they did. They'd asked what she likes to play with because they could buy two toys for her. Then they asked me what I needed and that was so unexpected. I was really touched. And while pride usually kept me from saying what I really need, all I thought to tell them was that I could really use a toaster. She asked if I needed a nice robe, and although that sounded really nice, I said no. I asked for a toaster. It was true that I needed one. I left the only one I'd ever had at the house and hadn't bought a new one because I couldn't decide if I wanted a cheapy, if I wanted a fancy one with four slots for making lots of toast at once, or if I wanted one that was part of a set. I saw a red one in Wal-Mart that I liked. Came with a coffee maker, and a blender. But then I didn't want to be limited to red kitchen decorations. I think you get a sense of why I've never bought one. Indecision and not wanting to be committed kept me from doing lots of things at the house. Those two things, plus feeling like I didn't have the money to do want I really wanted to do. So, I'd get to finding cheap, really cheap substitutions that never really last long or did exactly what I want them to do. I really needed a toaster, though, because I'd been trying to make toast in the oven with the broiler and would end up burning it, setting off the alarm, and having to fan my broom in front of the smoke detector to make it stop. I was getting tired of that routine.

So, when I got off the phone with the couple that night, two weeks ago, I was watching a Christmas special, I believe, and doing some schoolwork, tears began to flow. God works, I thought. He was working. This, I'd always known, but I don't think I'd ever seen the signs so clearly before now. I had been worried about Christmas, knowing that once I pay my bills this month, the ones I can pay this month, that there wouldn't be any money left for me to buy gifts for her. And then this couple called.

When we ended the conversation, they told me they'd get back in touch to make arrangements to deliver the items. They called on Sunday night, and I didn't take the call. I didn't quite know what to tell them and was worried, and maybe uncomfortable, at the thought of welcoming them back in my home again. Just because of pride. And not quite knowing how to react. And still not knowing how exactly to receive. Anything. I'm not a crier or a hugger, but this night, I hugged, at least. What they'd done was simple—they remembered me.

When they rang the doorbell, I was reluctant to answer, because we rarely have visitors, primarily because of the untidy house and cheap substitutions. I peered out the doorbell and immediately recognized Mr. Spokes. I opened the door, gave the warmest welcome I could, and apologized for the delay in answering. He said his wife called two nights in a row, and they thought they'd stop by because they really wanted to get our gifts to us. He said his wife was downstairs, he'd get her and the box and will be right back.

I shut the door, put on a better shirt and was just nervous, elated, and in disbelief.

"Who is it?" She came over from the table to ask likely because she also knows we don't have many visitors.

"Some people who'd helped us before had something for us. It's a surprise!"

She had on her pajamas and immediately, she put on those pink polka-dotted espadrilles with the bow on the front that she'd been wearing lately to play "teacher" with her babies.

"I'm going to put my shoes on to be ready."

In her excited anticipation, I don't think she knew quite what else to do. So, she put on her shoes, I changed my shirt, and we waited. I listened by the door for footsteps. When I heard none, I peeked out the window, looking three floors down, but I didn't see him. He said he'd be right back up. I wished I'd had some pink shoes to put on as well.

Finally, I heard the footsteps, and I opened the door before they could knock or ring the bell. Mr. Spokes had a great box. I was expecting three gifts. They had a huge box. Mr. Spokes asked me if he could speak to me outside for just a moment. He had a question for me in private, he said. I didn't quite know what he needed to know, but I hoped it wasn't anything heavy, with me not being a crier and all.

He smiled, and asked simply, "Do you mind Barbie?"

And then I heard a click. At first, it didn't register, the simplicity of his question, because I was expecting something heavy. I knew parents who didn't want their preschool children playing with a toy that had breasts, so I understood why Mr. Spokes asked the question.

"That's fine, that's absolutely fine," I said because she already has some Barbies. I was relieved that the question wasn't too deep but realized that that click at the door was my child locking me out of the house.

In the calmest voice I could find—even though I was nervous, because I was in my hang-around-the-house-clothes, with no keys and because I didn't want her to panic in realizing what she'd done because she's not so great with doors and locks, which I am proud of, sort of, because that meant she wouldn't ever be leaving the house unless I'm aware of it, but not so proud because if she ever needed to run for help, we'd be dead—I said, "Sweetie, open the door. Unlock the top lock."

And, praise God, she did.

The couple came in and set the box down, and I didn't exactly know what to say, except thank you and thank you again and thank you again. I hugged Mrs. Spokes, but no tears came. So, then I hugged Mr. Spokes. Still tearless. My kiddo was watching all of this, standing there in her pink shoes, with her purple high-water pajama pants, which I've convinced myself are supposed to be that length, watching all of this. Finally, I introduced her to them. I knew they'd been anxious to meet her because she wasn't home the last time they came.

It was a little awkward after this introduction was done, and I was glad that we'd put up our tree right after Thanksgiving. The couple may have sensed the awkwardness, but I knew they hadn't planned to really sit down and stay awhile and just then, they said they'd be heading off. We said our good-byes in the doorway, and Mrs. Spokes motioned for me to turn really quickly, in time to see my child trying to open one of the gifts. I closed the door, took the gift from her hand, and reassured her Christmas would be here in eight days. She threw a small tantrum, declaring she didn't want to wait, but she got over it quickly, and I looked at the box again. I emptied out the box and set five wrapped presents, one gift bag, and two cards underneath that tree.

By now she was already back at the table watching Dora. I walked through the living room over to her, just to look at her. She was in her own world again, pretending her fingers were crab claws like the baby crab on the summer *Dora* video. I walked through the kitchen, still feeling the impact of what just happened, I walked into my room. What happened was that they remembered me. And by *them*, I mean God. I'd been praying that Christmas would work out for her somehow. Not for me, but for her, just so that she could have something, one thing. And it did. And all I could do, in not knowing what to do, was to kneel by my bedside, and pray a prayer of thanks.

And then the tears came. I allowed myself to receive.

lord forgive me

lord forgive me
for all the wrong I've done
for not holding my tongue
for all the words I've said
for all the love I've refused to give
for all the words I should've said
for all the love I've refused to accept
for all the grudges I've kept
for being afraid to trust you
for not listening to you
for not following my heart
for getting hasty starts
lord forgive me for being so vain
forgive me for withholding so much pain
for not leaning on you
for wasting so much time
for asking for what shouldn't be mine
for asking for handouts
for not taking the time to figure You out
lord forgive me for everything
and please help me to rise up again
and walk with pride, but not too much
keep me humble
help me not to rush
all things will come naturally
what is meant to be will be
and You know what is meant for me
in your hands lies my destiny
but I realize you need help from me
to get going, to be motivated
forgive me lord for all those I've hated

forgive me for all my jealousy
for what they have was not meant for me
forgive me for my infidelity
forgive me for temptuous thoughts
forgive me for all the fights I've fought
forgive me for being me
for I am full of deficiencies,
but with You here to help me,
I know I can overcome.

be not anxious

(Transcription From a Church Address)

Phillippians 4:6-7 "Do not be anxious about anything, but in everything, by prayer and petition, with thanksgiving, present your requests to God…And the peace of God, which transcends understanding will guard your hearts and your mind in Christ Jesus."

When I listened to the sister's voice message, you have no idea how fast I hung up the phone! Talk about anxiety! Me doing this right now is the epitome of anxiety. Despite my current job and past job, I still have issues with talking in front of people. I am nervous. And you will know it when I start to stutter. My mom will say I've done this ever since I was a child. She could always tell I was lying because I would stutter. And, I'm not one to talk much about me. So, this is really going to be hard because what I intend to do is to give a bit of a personal testimony. If I do this without crying, then I'll be good.

At any rate, when I listened to her message, she said my name came up and I started thinking, are they sure they want me to do this? Then, I started thinking about all the reasons why I couldn't do this talk—all the reasons why I was wrong for this. In talking to my mom and one of my substitute teachers, who happens to be a pastor, I received good advice. Pastor and our first lady gave me reassurance that God wouldn't allow me to fail at this. What mom had to say was that if the church were seeking perfect people to speak, then no one could ever do it. Additional wisdom that I received included this: "You can do it. Do your preparation, but whatever comes out is what was meant to be." So, the message that I was hearing was that, with God, I can do this. And so, I'm praying now that God takes over and controls what is to come out of my mouth. That's one reason why I don't say much because my filter isn't that great. I want to be sure what comes out of my mouth is good.

I do want to note that I didn't sleep last night. I have major anxiety. That's why this is so good for me. I am truly facing one of my fears. For two years, I trained poll workers and then call center workers, and I would never be as nervous in training those individuals as I would when it came time to train other trainers. Those were my peers, and they would know when I messed up. And, so I am nervous today, because you are my peers, in a sense. You know as much as I do and more about scripture and you'll know when I mess up so, pray for me right now please.

I accepted this task because God has been too good to me not to try. And, my mom said that you can't give a talk like this unless you've been through something. And, lately, I've been through much. And prayer has strengthened me through it. Everything in my life right now is changing all at once—career, address, marital status. Even my daughter has a new school. Major transitions all at once. Without prayer and without God, I would have lost it by now. Right now, I am under God's mercy and grace. And when I think about the things I've struggled with just over the past year—the way things have lined up so perfectly—it's just amazing.

How do you feel when God has moved on your behalf?

It's through prayer that God can move for us. And all prayer is is communicating with God. For you moms, have you ever had a child decide they weren't going to speak to you? How did that feel?

That's exactly how God feels when we don't pray. I hear some folks say dad is their best friend or mom is their best friend. God wants to be that. Just like we talk to our best girlfriend, God is always there. And so, there are three main reasons I think, that we should pray:

1. To have a relationship. One of the main ways we keep relationships going is by talking. Ever been upset with your spouse and decided you weren't going to talk to them? That relationship is stifled. It can't go anywhere. We get to know God by talking to him, and he gets to know us as well. God wants to be our best girlfriend; the one you tell everything to. Communication keeps relationships going. You can't have a relationship with God if you can't talk to Him. Earlier on, I started talking to God by doing what pastor suggested long ago: talking to God no matter where you are or what you're doing—watching TV, in the car—wherever you are you can stop and talk to God. However, now, I wake up in the morning and give him my full attention, and I've found when I give Him my full attention and pray before I get too sleepy to focus on Him, that that is when I am helped the most, that is when His voice is clearest. The life of Jesus is the best example of this for me. Jesus prayed to God for direction in everything he did. (Mark 14:34-41 and Matthew 26:36-39).

2. To recognize who God is. He is the Creator. And, I like the way one song put it: He is the creator of all that you see. Just look around. Every single thing you see: God created it. And I think that's awesome. We ought to recognize Him just for that. No one else can do what he does. In my traveling training job, I really got to understand this better as I was in Colorado, driving in the mountains and in Hawaii, looking at the ocean. The mountains and the ocean scare me because they are bigger than me. Anything that's bigger than me scares me. I can't stand next to a plane. Standing next to buildings scare me. Things that are bigger than me, especially things in nature, scare me because they remind me

of how big God is and of how mighty He is. For me, Psalms 96 put this best. It starts, "Sing to the Lord a new song, praise His name, declare His glory day after day…." This is where supplication and thanksgiving comes in. Humbling ourselves before Him and thanking Him for who he is.

3. To seek direction from God. This is a big one for me. I really didn't learn how to do this, truly, until last summer when I started all these major life transitions. You can't hear from someone unless you talk to them. If we want God's advice, we must talk to Him about it. About it all. And so, I've started telling God everything and praying over everything. Several months ago, I bought my daughter a fish, and I found myself praying over this little stinky fish, that it won't die so that I won't have to explain to my child what happened to the fish. I complain to God about the colleagues that get on my nerves. And nine times of out 10 He reveals something to me that I need to do better. But I would never have gotten that feedback unless I brought the problem to Him in prayer. Psalms 94:19 reads "When anxiety was great within me, your consolation brought joy to my soul."

Are there any other reasons that we should pray? How about for peace? For healing? For mercy?

In doing a little research about prayer, I came across some reasons why it may seem like prayers go unanswered. This I found really interesting:

1. Unforgiveness. Mark 11:22-25 reads, *"But when you are praying, first forgive anyone you are holding a grudge against, so that your Father in heaven will forgive your sins to."*

2. Pride. 2 Chronicles 7:14-15 reads, *"Then if my people who are called by my name will humble themselves and pray and*

seek my face and turn from their wicked ways, I will hear from heaven and will forgive their sins and heal their land."

3. Greed. James 4:2-3 reads, *"You want what you don't have, so you scheme and kill to get it. You are jealous for what others have, and you can't possess it, so you fight and quarrel to take it away from them. And yet the reason you don't have what you want is that you don't ask God for it. And even when you do ask, you don't get it because your whole motive is wrong—you want only what will give you pleasure."*

4. Stubbornness. Zechariah 7:11-13 reads, *"Your ancestors would not listen to this message. They turned stubbornly away and put their fingers in their ears to keep from hearing. They made their hearts as hard as stone, so they could not hear the law or the messages that the LORD Almighty had sent them by his Spirit through the earlier prophets. That is why the LORD Almighty was so angry with them. Since they refused to listen when I called to them, I would not listen when they called to me, says the LORD Almighty."*

So, if it seems like we've been praying and praying on one thing that just won't be overcome or go away, we must step back to see if we have any of these prayer-blockers in the way—greed, stubbornness, selfishness, pride.

Pride is a huge one for me and one of the reasons why I started thinking that I can't do this. Not wanting to reveal anything about myself because of pride. However, when you have children, especially little children, I've found that they tell all your business anyway. It seems like gone are the days of "what happens in this house stays in this house." Anyone ever grow up hearing that? I did. But these days, that's dangerous, I feel. I don't want my child to feel afraid of ashamed to talk about anything. And, I feel if I was woman enough to do it or say it in front of her, then I should be woman enough to let her tell it. That didn't come out right, but I basically do not want to encourage my child to keep secrets. Secrets can be toxic. And what I have just recently learned is that what I'm going through may have a lesson for me in it, but what I'm going through or have been through is not just for me. It's for me to share to someone else to testify to God's goodness and faithfulness. My experiences are to help someone else along.

So now that I've talked about prayer, let me say a little about being anxious. I was anxious about talking to you today. Did I mention that I didn't sleep? When I looked the word up, the definition read "anticipation of future events or exaggerated desire or a state of uncertainty" or just plain "fear."

What are some things that we get anxious about? I'm anxious for my daughter to start kindergarten so that I won't have to pay these private pre-school fees! I'm anxious about my students taking the TAKS test! I'm anxious about spring break! I'm anxious about being better off financially!

I suffer from anxiety. So much so that about two years ago, when I started this traveling training job and was facing my fear of talking in front of groups of people and dealing with leaving my child for a few days at a time, I sought medical advice. My doctor gave me Paxil. I can't really say if it ever really helped me back then because I couldn't ever remember to take it every day. But just last summer, I found myself needing it again.

During this major transition, I was feeling overwhelmed and anxious. I mean, I was sweating. Literally. I started a new job, teaching, and newly separated, I was pretty much living as a single mom. For any of you single moms, now I know how you do it—you do it because you have to. There is no other alternative. There is no one else to do it. But it's God's grace and strength that gives you the power.

So, I would wake up in the morning to get ready for work and be sweating. Sweat running down my legs. I'd shower at night and have to shower again in the morning because by the time I'd have my daughter ready, I'd be sweating. I was feeling anxious about being late for work. And feeling overwhelmed with starting a new job, having to work more than 40 hours to learn the ropes, trying to fit in time to play with my daughter and clean the house. And when the job was going well, my home was a mess. And when my home was straight, my job wasn't going well. I was stressed.

And sometimes, I'd get nervous about teaching the students. At first, the students were tough on me. They have stolen from me all their positive rewards, which is too bad for them because they still have to do the work, they just won't get rewarded for it. They were behaving horribly and at one point I had lost my confidence.

In order for me to relax a bit in the morning and not be so hot and sweaty, I was taking a Benadryl in the morning. You know how you take it when you have allergies, and it makes you drowsy? Well, I would take one, even though I wasn't suffering from allergies, and it didn't make me drowsy. Somehow, it balanced me…for a little while. I would get through the work week and then on Saturdays find that my house was a mess, that I needed to play with my daughter, grade papers, plan lessons, etc, etc, etc, and I was still overwhelmed. Until one morning, I got up, looked at all the dishes in the sink and realized I had all this cleaning to do, and I was tired. No strength left. My daughter was playing in her room. I went into mine and got on my knees to pray. And I asked God to help me prioritize my stuff, and I asked Him to help me not feel guilty about the things that I didn't get done.

This was such a humbling moment for me because I couldn't even tell you the last time I had gotten down on my knees to pray— to truly pray and acknowledge that I cannot do it through my own will, and that I needed God's help to order my life.

I had to make lists in order for me to remember what I needed to do. My memory is pretty much shot, and I'm just 34—I think bad memory is hereditary. But I'd cross these things off my lists as I'd finish, and if by the end of the day, I still had stuff on my list that I didn't do, I'd feel like a loser. I had to ask God to take that away from inside me and to be satisfied that my day went according to His will. But since that day on my knees, I haven't had to pop a Benadryl. I certainly started looking for some this morning, though!

When I think about being anxious in terms of prayer, I think of getting ahead of God. Of asking God to do something and not allowing Him to do it, of not spending enough time in conversation about it with God, and/or confusing our own will with the will of God.

But I've come to realize that there's no need and no good in worrying. When we worry, it's like doubting God. And doubt is one of those prayer-blockers. God created the entire world, surely, He's powerful enough to take care of our needs.

Through reading and prayer, one thing that I find powerful and that still moves me to tears is that God has not forgotten about me. About us. It's in His word. I become moved when I realize that the Creator of the world knows me and hasn't forgotten about me. My point is that surely, if He can keep the oceans from flooding the land, surely, He can take care of our needs. God can do it. We just have to let Him. Psalms 139 begins, "Oh Lord, you have searched me and you know me…"

A scripture that helped me through this difficult summer and my trying Christmas break is Psalms 40. It is a prayer for help written by David. The structure of this prayer is awesome. He doesn't just say, "Lord, please help me." He started out by praising God for all his mercy. Then he professes his commitment to do God's will, then he praises God for who He is and then finally, David asks for help. I love this Psalm. It has helped me tremendously. For several months, I would wake up and read it each morning. And just be in tears as God spoke to me through his word. One morning, my daughter came in my room and after seeing me reading my bible and crying over a period of time, she asked me, "Mama, does the bible make you hurt?" And I had to explain to her that I cry because God has been so good and that our blessings come from God.

I have two more thoughts on prayer and being anxious. One is truly a thought and the other is a story. When I was asked to talk today, I was nervous not just because I had to speak in front of you, but also because of some difficulty I'm having in my marriage a relatively young marriage—it will soon be nine years. I keep in touch with a group of women that I've known for a long time, who are also in young marriages and trying to be good Christians. What's on my mind is the state of young marriages and young men and young women. Based on my own experience and those other young women that I know, it seems that they are in trouble.

When I stated that what I'm going through isn't just for me, this is part of what I was referring to. Young wives right now are having to pray their husbands out of things like pornography, alcohol, clubbing, working too much, praising money and not God, verbal abuse, and infidelity. Some young women are dealing with young husbands who haven't had Godly male role models and so, they don't really know what a Christian husband is supposed to be like. And, too many of us young women in these young marriages are being too silent. Young marriages need a whole lot of prayer and so, I'm asking that you pray for young marriages and that you pray that young married people won't be too anxious and make rash decisions.

Lastly, here's my story regarding not being anxious and allowing God to work it out. I have a car that was about five years old last year. One of the things that I was stressed about was the fact that my car wasn't acting right. In the mornings it would start really hard when I'd turn the ignition and sometimes it'd buck like a horse and sometimes the engine would run, but the car wouldn't move at all when I pressed the gas. I was nervous. I was at a new job, I needed to get to my students to teach them, I needed to make this money, and my car was acting up.

I didn't know what could be wrong, except I figured it was either an engine problem or shifting problem. My budget was so tight that I couldn't really afford to fix whatever was wrong. The car is a Hyundai, and they have the fabulous warranty, 10 years/ 100,000 miles, but I figured that I'd still have to pay something just to have them look at it, and I was afraid of what they'd find. So, I prolonged taking it to be looked at.

Meanwhile, sometimes I'd get all set to drive to work and my daughter and I would be sitting in the car with the engine running, just waiting for the car to decide to move. It had a mind of its own. Then, it started not wanting to come out of reverse so, I had to start backing into parking spots so I wouldn't have to use reverse; I could just drive. On several occasions, while driving to work and even to church, my car would start and even drive down the road, but if I stopped for a stoplight or stop sign, the car would just sit there running, even though I was pressing the gas, until it was ready to move. I was nervous.

So, I started thinking what if this car stops running, what will I do? It'd be dangerous for my daughter, and I to be walking on the side of the road. And, sometimes I wear a small heel to work, there's no way I could walk for help in those, and she's so little, she's gonna get tired quickly.

Then, I thought I could just call for help, if necessary, and just sit in the car for someone to drive to me, in the event the car stopped. I would drive out to the suburbs either on the toll road or on the back-country roads, in either case there aren't any gas stations and not many passers-by.

So, I would drive and pray from home to work and from work to home and from home to church and back, and I felt a little safer knowing I had my cell phone. And usually, once the car got going, it was fine. Highway driving was good. It was just getting the car started up.

I talked to my mom about the situation, and you know how mothers worry. So, she asked my uncle if he would look at my car and price out repairs and everything. So, he started doing some research and thought that maybe I needed a tune-up. Do you know I'd never had a tune up on this car? Never. From what I knew about tune ups, they can be expensive, and I immediately thought I couldn't afford that.

When my mom told me to call my uncle and work out a time for him to check it out, I told her I could not afford the $200 he said it'd cost for a tune up. Well, then she said she'd pay for it; she just wanted me to be safe. She told me to call him.

I didn't. I kept praying. I was praying and driving all the way to work in the morning. And since work is in the east, I'd be driving into the sunrise in the morning. And I felt like it was just me and God, and I'd have my gospel music on, and the sun would be beaming in my eyes, and I'd be praying, "Please, Lord, get me to this school."

And my uncle called a few times to catch up with me, and I didn't return his calls.

Then one morning, my security was gone; my cell phone stopped working. However, I still had to get to work every day and I only had one car to get in to get there. I was praying hard then for a solution, for protection, to not get stranded and to get to work on time. I felt as though I were being tested, big time. Here I am in a new job, all these transitions, and now my car is acting up, and my phone is shutting down. What am I to do?

This was about October or so, so I started praying that I could, that my car could make it to Christmas break, that way I could have some time and some money to have it checked out. And it did. I just knew that God wouldn't put me in this new job, and then take away my means of getting to it.

During the break, though, I was not ready to move in the direction of my uncle, even though my mom said she'd help me out and cover the costs. It seemed like a done deal. My uncle who knows about cars would check it out and do the work, and mom would pay for it. They were waiting on me to say the word so they could get to work, but I couldn't agree to it. Something was telling me that that wasn't the solution.

During the break, I started flipping through the owner's manual and remembered that this fabulous warranty that Hyundai advertises was still in place for my car. I had about 98,000 miles on it, and the warranty expires at 100,000. God's grace. I flipped through the manual more and learned that if the problem was as I suspected, it would be covered under warranty. God's mercy. I called up Aamco, not yet wanting to deal with the dealership. They checked it out and told me just what I needed to hear: the problem was a transmission axel seal leaking oil. My transmission had no oil. No wonder the car wouldn't start. Hearing this, I finally called the dealership. Praying the whole time that I would be dealing with a patient and honest employee. Over the phone, they told me that I needed proof of registration. This was on December 30. My registration was to expire on December 31. My budget was tight, and I really hadn't planned on paying that registration on time, but the way things worked out, it was meant for me to pay. God's grace. I had just enough in my budget to pay the registration so I could give the dealership proof that I was the original car owner.

Being up against the New Year's Eve closures and celebrations, I felt as though God showed up for me just in time. I worked with two repairmen as they fixed my car; both were polite and honest. The first repairman confirmed what Aamco said—it was a seal. And they also confirmed that it was covered under warranty. God's grace.

Now, the first repairmen said that I might have to pay them about $60 for the oil they would put in the transmission because it was bone dry. Although, I had just gotten oil changed at Wal-Mart, and they told me it was fine. However, when they called me back to let me know the part had arrived, and when I brought my car for the repair, they charged me nothing at all. It was all under warranty. The only thing I paid for is my registration renewal. I haven't expressed this situation well enough to really describe just how much of a blessing this has been.

I think the two things that I pray most often about are my finances and balancing work with home life. Three—also my daughter's well-being. One quick story about getting ahead of God and being anxious goes like this.

I had been juggling a couple of bills over the last several months and had been under God's grace and mercy with working it all out. I was praying about it and trusting God, and things were working out. However, I decided to move ahead of God one day, feeling tired of doing this juggling act. So, I'm grocery shopping and shopping as I'm hungry, which is a no-no and I kept putting things in the basket and as I was walking down the aisles, I knew that I was going over my budget. My inner voice was telling me to stop shopping, you have enough, time to go. But I decided my budget could handle it knowing that I might be over and that maybe I could "float" a check or something. So, I bought the groceries. I had a carload, too. Drove home and when I stepped inside my house the lights were off, which meant no frig to put all these cold foods in. My point is that God puts us where we are for a reason—He wants us to budget accordingly and to tithe—and sometimes the things we do to ourselves, puts us where we are, and perhaps God chooses to keep us there His reasons. We have no idea what He is working out on our behalf way over there on the other side. Getting ahead of Him when we already put it in His hands can mess things up. Working in our own strength can also mess things up.

> *Philippians 4:6-7: Do not be anxious about anything, but in everything, by prayer and petition, with thanksgiving, present your requests to God…And the peace of God, which transcends understanding will guard your hearts and your mind in Christ Jesus.*

God doesn't want you to worry. Worry and anxiety cancel each other out. When you truly give it to God, you have peace about it, whatever it is. God wants you to trust him to work it out. We ask Him to work it out through relationship, through communication, through prayer. It's through all of these situations, big and small, that I've learned to pray. And perhaps that was the point, His purpose for the struggles all along.

joy isn't cyclical

There are moments when life becomes so clear—there are moments when my thinking becomes so clear, and I can see how things fit together and how my life is supposed to be just as it is, and how I am actually moving in the right direction and the feeling is like what I imagine a high to be—feeling so full and my heart starts racing. Then I imagine that that's what it feels like when you're touched by the spirit of God—but then I always get scared in those moments.

Those bursts of happiness scare me so badly, part of me feels as though since things are becoming so clear, that I'm actually able to make some sense of life, that mine must be coming to an end, and this scares me because I haven't yet lived the way I want to live or done the things I want to do. I realize that it is absurd to think that knowledge is only for the dead and dying, and confusion is for the living.

But those moments of clarity also scare me because the little moments of happiness, moments of fullness are so rare that they feel unfamiliar, they feel strange, they feel out of place, and I don't have control of them, so I tend to run back to the familiar confusion.

Fear keeps us running back to what is familiar and what is safe, and this is so wrong. Acting in fear instead of in faith can lead to big mistakes. Courage is doing, moving, speaking, going forward even though you're scared. Faith is trusting even though you can't see what's ahead.

In reading Hebrews last week, I was really moved. God is not happy with us when we step out on the ledge of faith and then run back away from the edge because we're scared. In those moments, we demonstrate a lack of faith. And usually, or for me, at least, what follows is guilt. Guilt because I lost faith and didn't trust that my life is not happening on my own strength and power, but by the strength and power, plus mercy and grace of God. I think when we shrink back in fear, that signifies that we think we can't do it. And that part is true. *We* can't do it. Not alone. We *need* His help.

I also think that it's strange that, for me, what feels familiar is confusion and not clarity, fear and not courage, heartache and not happiness, worry and not trust. I'd bet that would sadden Jesus as well—that what feels familiar and comfortable are among the things He died to rid us of. However, what I'm realizing is that it's okay to be happy. It's okay to have moments of true joy, even if life hasn't worked out the way we planned it. We are not the real planners of life anyway.

It's okay to not be overtaken by guilt. It's okay to be happy, even if we've done things that we really should feel guilty about. It's okay to be happy even though we have unresolved pain or problems, to take some time to be happy because we have a Problem-bearer and Problem-solver who will work it out. Our time spent worrying is time spent in vain. Instead, perhaps we should take some time to be happy that we don't have to worry. Take some time to remember that our Savior lives, and He is in control.

There's a song that says something like "inside it feels like chaos, but I believe something's happening in me, that God is up to something." When things *feel* chaotic and out of control, chances are that's because they *really are* chaotic and out of control. One thing I'm dealing with is the notion of when will I have everything under control, when will I have everything in order. But the reality is that

I never will. Because I'm not in control, and I don't know what the order *is*. Only He does.

So, chances are the out-of-control feeling is real, and is present just to emphasize, just to underline the fact that <u>we aren't in control</u>. And for us to accept that fact. I think that's usually what God is up to. That he's reminding us that *He's* got this. He literally does. You know that song, 'He's Got the Whole World in His Hands"? So simple, but so true.

Moments of happiness shouldn't be few and far between. True joy shouldn't be fleeting and rare so much so that they make us scared and uncomfortable. Those moments shouldn't make us feel unworthy, which is often what happens to me. I feel undeserving of such true joy. But we have to remember that there's no way we can earn our joy. There's nothing we can do, no act we can perform, no prayer we can pray, nothing we can give up that is enough to earn joy or God's grace or mercy. So, also in those moments when we feel we've overcome, when we feel we have the victory—and don't get me wrong, I've had many of those, especially within the last year— we shouldn't get to thinking that we've overcome because of something that we did. We shouldn't get too proud of ourselves. We should feel victorious because God worked it out, because He fought for us, because He interceded on our behalf, because He stepped in a right on time, because He saved the day, literally. There's nothing we can do to be worthy of such loving kindness, of true mercy and unselfishness. There is no sacrifice we have to make, no sacrifice we *could* make. His mercy and kindness and forgiveness run freely and abundantly through the blood of Christ.

We are imperfect because we are not Him. We are imperfect because we need Him. He loves us in all our wonderful imperfections. He already knows every single one of them because He created every single one of us. We don't have to be sitting in a church for God to see us, know us, hear us. There's nothing that we do that goes unseen. There's nothing that we say that goes unheard. There's nothing that we think that goes unknown. If only more of us could grasp this.

I had a student who would come in everyday and cover his head with his hood. It was as if he felt that as long as he couldn't see me that I couldn't see him. It seems that's the way many of us walk around—thinking that we're hiding from God. That as long as we don't seek Him, don't read the bible, don't go to church, don't pray that he can't see us. Nothing could be more untrue. He's always, always there. Always was, always will be. And he wants us to be happy, but the only way to be happy is through the joy that's found in Him. And His joy, once we place it inside, is forever. It's permanent. Joy shouldn't be cyclical like the moon or waves. Joy is steady, joy is constant, like the air. We just must look inward and focus on Him to know that joy is always present regardless of what's going on around us. It, like love, is not a feeling that comes and goes as it wishes. It's always there but we must act to connect to it. We have to actively seek it to connect to it and to sustain it. And, according to my faith, the only way is through Christ—coming with Him, getting closer to Him, and allowing Him to live in us.

begin again

If I could begin again,
I would take the world out of your perfect plan
If I could begin again,
I would not have asked the world
 when I was trying to understand
If I could begin again,
I would have trusted
that it would come to pass in your time
If I could begin again,
I would not ignore the signs
Forgive me Lord for standing in the middle of Your work,
for trying to speed You along,
for thinking that I knew what was best,
for thinking, "I've got this,"
for allowing my will to overtake Yours and
for my time to be more important than Yours
I just keep thinking of Joshua and Caleb
And I wonder how badly I've messed up
What blessing won't come to fruition
All because I decided that I knew what was best
If I could begin again,
I'd let my patience endure
Please flush away the guilt within
Please rid me of these acts of sin
Please erase the feeling of stupidity
That is written all over me
I feel as though everyone can see
The worst parts of me
Lord, please try me again, please test me again
Lord, please let me begin again.
This time, I aim to win
In you, I can overtake the sin.

church

the only place that I can go to
find peace
in this chaos I call life—the
only place where I can feel
complete calm
and genuine joy.
where everyone around me is moving and I
am still
so it seems.

big ole buts

(Transcription From a Church Address)

But I don't spend enough time with my kids.
But I don't cook enough.
But my house isn't clean enough.
BUT I didn't finish school.
But I dropped out of school.
But I didn't get the job.
But I'm getting old.
But I don't have the right dresses.
But I've had an abortion.
But I still enjoy clubbing.
But I've gained too much weight.
But I pushed their father away.
But I live with my parents.
But I still don't have a husband.
But I knew it would happen, and I did it anyway.
But I knew it would happen, and I let them do it anyway.
But if only I was there, it would not have happened.
But I'm not smart enough.
But I can't pay my bills.
But I knew he was married.
But if I tell the truth, what will they think?
But I was fired.
But I don't know enough scripture.
But it was my fault that he hit me.
But I gave up my children.

Big old buts. We need to lose some weight ladies. The Lord don't want our buts. God don't want our buts; He wants our commitments and whole hearts. These buts keep getting in the way! Of doing His work. They weigh us down. We have fallen on our buts and cannot get up! We have found nice, soft excuses to go with our buts, and now we're glued to them.

Donnie McClurkin sings *"We fall down, but we get up… For a saint is just a sinner who fell and got up!"*

A saint. All the saints are just sinners *who had the sense enough to get up*!

We are so deep in our self-centered, self-induced pity party that we can't see what God has intended to do with our mistakes, situations, detours! They are *all* meant for His *glory*.

Genesis 50:20 says, *"But as for you, you meant evil against me; but God meant it for good…"* *The saints got up, meaning they repented.* Guilt can be good. Guilt can serve a purpose. Guilt can lead us to God, if we can look past ourselves and forward to conviction. John 16:8 says, *"And when (the Holy Spirit) comes, He will convict the world concerning sin, and righteousness, and judgment."* We can't get up unless and until we *repent*. The Holy Spirit dwells in the hearts of the saved to convict us when we do wrong so we can get right with God.

A diamond isn't born,
its formed
refined under pressure
and heat.

There is a delicate balance between holding on and letting go. This became clear to me the other day when I was teaching my daughter to ride her bike.

Holding on creates dependence.
Think about that baby that sleeps in your bed too long or
the baby who lays on your chest too long or
sucks on the bottle too long, or
if we take medications for too long, or
keep the training wheels on too long…

it becomes hard to let go.
Provides comfort, a handy excuse, a dependence.
Hold on to guilt too long and
it becomes shame.

Yet, shame is not from God. There is no condemnation in God.

Romans 8:1 says, *"Therefore, there is now no condemnation for those who are in Christ Jesus. Believe and be released."* Imagine how great we'd be without these big old buts!

That's why Jesus came. To provide a way out and a way up off our buts. We sometimes won't let ourselves forget who we used to be or what we don't have or what we've done or what we've allowed to be done to us. Satan sucks us back into the very sin that Jesus delivered us from.

I say turn the tables on Satan and *use* that sin as a **test**imony. 2 Timothy 1:7-8 says, *"For God did not give us a spirit of timidity, but a spirit of power, of love and of self-discipline. So do not be ashamed to testify about our Lord…".* Luke 8:39 says, *"The man from whom the demons had gone out begged to go with him, but Jesus sent him away, saying, "Return home and tell how much God has done for you." So, the man went away and told all over town how much Jesus had done for him."* Our **test**imonies don't belong to us, they belong to God. They are about God and for God, to **test**ify to whomever will listen about how we took the test, and in some cases, took the test *and* retook the test, until we *finally* passed.

So, here is just a little piece of my testimony: I used to be a cursing, clubbing "Christian." I do actually have a little shame about that now because my mama is here listening, and I don't think she had ever heard my filthy mouth. But the fact remains, I used to be a cursing, clubbing "Christian," plus a drinking and fornicating "Christian." Satan would love to have kept me bound to those butts, but there's no denying who I am now. Now I'm saved and among the saints and a servant who be trying to sing the gospel! There's no denying God's deliverance. If you've accepted Jesus, you are a saint, too. Let's quit telling ourselves we are less than that.

Shame is not from God. Pastor preached on the devil's tools last week. Shame is another tool the devil uses to dig a trench between us and God. Eve gave us an example of what happens when we listen to Satan. Genesis 3:12-13 says, *"The man said, 'The woman you put here with me—she gave me some fruit from the tree, and I ate it.'"* Then the LORD God said to the woman, "What is this you have done?" The woman said, "The serpent deceived me, and I ate." Listening to Satan produces disobedience, influencing others to sin, shame, and, if we don't give it to Jesus, death.

God doesn't intend for us to wallow in shame, have a pity party, cry in the dark. Holding on to guilt is a sign that we don't *believe*; don't *believe* God died to carry all our sin; don't *believe* that we are worthy of forgiveness, that we are *worthy* of better, that we are *worthy* of love, that we have God on our side ready to offer forgiveness; don't believe that we've already been forgiven, because we asked Him way back when, but we decided we could carry that sin better than Jesus can!

1 John 4:9 says, *"This is how God showed his love among us: He sent his one and only Son into the world that we might live through him."* God wants our praise, and He wants to love us! Not just our *good* parts, or those parts we deem to be *good, all* of us!

There are moments when I ashamed of the pieces of me.
Not the whole,
but the pieces—the pieces of me that were used improperly,
impulsively, unwisely,
indiscretionally,
Improperly.
There are pieces that I wish would fall off
completely.
But these pieces, they make up me.

They belong to me
define me
compose me.
I am them and they are me
indefinitely.
However, God has already forgiven me
for those little pieces that shame me
and I don't want to shame Thee
by continually feeling shamefully
about these little pieces that define me;
for the definition of your forgiveness is to believe and be set free
and therefore, I am not defined by me but by Thee and
in Thee
and for that I have no shame. Thank you, Lord,
for reminding me daily
that, in you, I can live wholly
all because I surrendered my everything to Thee.
Thank you for allowing your body to hang brokenly
so that, in you, mine could have a new shame-free assembly.
Thank you, Lord, for wholly loving me—
every little broken piece.

He wants to love *all* of us! Not just our good parts, *all of us!* Psalms 138:1 says, *"I will praise thee, O Lord, with my whole heart!"* We are to take it to God and pour it on *Him*. Psalms 25:42 says, *"Cast your cares on the LORD and he will sustain you; he will never let the righteous fall."* That's what He was born for. It's written on our church wall!

He was born, died, and rose to take on the sin of the *world*. But we have to give it to Him and *leave* it with Him. It seems some us of only let Him borrow our sin—we give it to Him for a little while, let Him *hold* it, and then we take it back.

Remember that song "Superwoman?" Came out in the 90s by Karen Whyte? *"I'm not your superwoman! Oh no, no, no, no."* We are not supposed to be superwomen. Not supposed to be super. Only One is, and He sits high. Karen Whyte goes on to say, *"I'm not the kind of girl that you can let down and think that everything is ok."* I think she meant this for man, but I'd like to think she was talking to the devil. We need to tell Satan that we are not the kind of girls that he can let down and think that everything is ok. Karen Whyte says, *"Boy, I am only human."* We are just that. We are fallible. There's not been perfection in humanity since Adam fell from grace. God's perfect work is our salvation.

God created woman with such care. Genesis 2:21-23 says:

"And the LORD God caused a deep sleep to fall upon Adam, and he slept: and he took one of his ribs and closed up the flesh instead thereof; And the rib, which the LORD God had taken from man, made he a woman, and brought her unto the man. And Adam said,' This is now bone of my bones, and flesh of my flesh: she shall be called Woman, because she was taken out of Man.'"

God thought so much of us, of our gender, that He sent the Savior of the world through one of us—man didn't have nothing to do with that! With God being all-powerful, He could have sent the Savior in any way He pleased; yet, He sent Him through a woman. Matthew 1:22-23 says, *"Behold, a virgin shall be with child, and shall bring forth a son, and they shall call his name Emmanuel, ...God with us."*

He has wonderful plans for us. God is calling women to walk with blameless assurance found in Him. John 10:27 says, *"My sheep listen to my voice. I know them and they follow me."* Let's lay down that guilt and shame that only Satan wants us to keep. Believe He died to bear it all, believe He wants us to live shame free, believe that you have His grace, believe that, like He did with the woman with the alabaster jar and like he did with Ester, He wants to complete a great work in our lives. But He needs us to get up our off buts!

There is no shame in God's game. The devil can have our minds wrapped up so tight that we *feel* like we can't let go of what we did, what we said, what we should have done. But God is a God who doesn't operate on how we *feel*. And with Him we can do all things!!! Philippians 4:13 says, *"I can do all things through Christ which strengtheneth me."* Trust Him and let's take our hands off it because we can't make it right anyway. We can't wash away our own sin. Tell your shame, "You're history!" Tell yourself, "I've got the victory!" Tell your mistakes, "You will be used for God's glory!" Trust Him, grab onto Him, and ask Him to pull us up off our big old buts!

you remain silent

you remain silent in his love like time—
it is silent, but it is passing, active, always moving you.
It is silent; moves you, like waves

rhythmic, unguided, you move through it,
float in it, calmly, like atmosphere.
you remain silent in his love like time—

intangible, like thoughts unspoken, private, ever-present, you
cannot see it, but it fills you,
sustains you, and surrounds you, like the breeze that
it is silent; moves you, like waves,

with power to engulf you, and ignite you like flames but it
thaws you and warms you like the sun that brightens and shines
upon you, and
you remain silent in his love like time

that consumed you as it drenches you, cleanses you,
dependable and faithful, cyclic, like the moon that
it is silent; moves you, like waves,

plentiful as the stars, shining—so much of it shining, it illuminates
you,
and it shines through you quietly as the time that passes, even
when you silently pass,
you remain silent in his love that remains like time.
that is silently moving you, like waves.

vitality

drifting down a boundless depression,
level off on an extension and

Dangle

for immeasurable moments,
languishing for salvation.
visage emerges from the incandescent cleft,
tender length of a twisted member extended.

Collapse.

bellowing in vain,
plunge into the somber abyss,
swirling so rapidly my utterance misses,
desperately needing to

Smack

the bleak underside so rigidly,
so irrevocably,
that the frame shakes,

Awakens.

my calling

I have found my calling
my creative me.
Activities that please me
and
let me be me
and let me
run free
fly free
think free
without boundaries.
No numbers or
calculators or formulas
or definitions.
Just lines and
circles and
words and
visions and
clicks and
space and
letters and
colors.
I have found me
and what I was
meant to be.
I have found my calling
my creative me.

"The monotony and solitude of a quiet life stimulates the creative mind."

— ALBERT EINSTEIN

next

"It is a great thing to know the season for speech and the season for silence."

— SENECA

second life

creativity
incubates in silence. art
anticipated

the first half of life
swiftly fades. with what's left, live
intentionally,

create with purpose.
let silence live loudly. You
found your voice. use it—

give life to your gift.
let your creativity
live and breathe and be

often. Your gift is
life, light, salt. Season us well.
life is fleeting.

journey through it well.
love well. speak well. learn well. write
more. write well. fear less.

listen more. listen:
honor silence well, express
conceptions therein

learned. life shortens with
realization that life ends.
second life, begin!

Coming Soon in Volume Two: Poetry from

l. smith

---

the sudden impact of June

All June,
I sly smile at Craftsman,
Gillette, Leatherman,
for my not being slumped into the same
road hole—
the grill, tool, tie, tech and meat-prep buying frenzy,
the man-caved, mind-bending commercial conundrum—
that the others have sunken into, until
that weekend,
the tip off of celebrations with
patriarchs, when
the hollow ache dropkicks my facade,
teeing up silent tears that dissolve my smirk,
leaving open and unguarded my
yearning
to strategize a gift for daddy
25 Father's Days post-cancer
mortem.

uncouth accolades

a joke
swung, in uncouth delight
on a prestigious and glamorous
night, but the butt's
Protector
delivered
the punchline
squarely
amid the famous,
and the evening's glitz
swatted low upon an
infamous zinger that
fell flatly.

Profane clamor.

A code broken?

An honor
defended? Or,
a mockery
made?

A purpose
lived? Or,
the wealthy
unwise?

A punchline delivered—
a jarring jab line centered
on the joke-teller's jaw—
and climatic indeed,
in the absence of laughter.

The famous now infamous? Or,
the legendary limelighted
in the
infamy
of humanity?

yoga in the park

In the park
On a mat
atop the winter grass
Under the bleached waves
which we call clouds,
I looked heavenward and
saw the sapphire water,
which we call sky, which is separated
from the land by His essence—synonymous for
the sustaining, still atmosphere.

I was cradled by His steady, intentional hands,
which we call gravity,
while I inhaled His transcending breath—a synonymity
of the invigorating, chilly air.

And, I was so grateful to then gaze
upon the heavens,
while I lay in reverse prostrate
upon a mat atop the winter grass,
so grateful, that for a moment,
while I lay there extended and motionless,
quietly, momentarily, I
cried,
amid the mothers from the land—
whether they had birthed
physical beings or not—
who lay motionless adjacent to me.

With momentary quivering lips,
I lay for a moment in the park
in melanated, stationary sisterhood,
overwhelmed by the beauty of the
water that we call the sky,
and overcome by the grace
of His breath
in my lungs, the
oxygen
that I respire mindfully, greedily—
that oxygen that can be exploited,
thoughtlessly, habitually—
the oxygen that we respire
in unanimity, purposefully.

I closed my eyes and within my forearms
stirred that bewitched tingle,
and not able to resist the urge—
that magnetic pull from the heavens—
my outstretched arms and holy hands
ascended in upturned prostrate praise,
spiritually symbolizing that I am open
to receive all that He has for me.

Overjoyed,
I opened my teary eyes for a moment more
to gaze again upon His beauty, that is the water we call sky,
and through the rolling waves, which we call drifting clouds—
through the glowing, gliding
alabaster clouds that He rendered
beautifully, momentarily motionless,
exclusively for me —
He privately fashioned the alluring clouds
into a graceful, buoyant, illuminating,
feminine formation

to show
me
me.

Surrounded by queens,
descendants from the motherland,
I felt a moving,
powerful and protective peace
that afforded me a timely, spirit-nourishing
affirmation and
the opportunity to just be
free
like the ancestors were in the Motherland,
and to be without worry for a
moment in the park
and to be without worry for a change
in the park,
while momentarily
extending my limbs in royal solidarity
for a soul
release,
on a mat atop the winter grass in the park,
under the protective watch of
the heavenly waters, which we call sky,
while I gazed upon the levitating waves,
which we call
clouds,
in solidarity
with the women
whom I call queens,
which we are,
because
God.

black dad matters

I come from a black man,
a black dad,
a real black dad,
a really loving black dad,
a black girl dad,
who was in my black home for my whole black life,
married to ***just***
my black mother—his black wife—all his adult black life
and his black life mattered—mattered dearly to me,
from his black life came mine and that of my black brother, and, in
turn, our black children, and so many black blessings and black
benefits and black lessons.
I come from a black man,
a black dad,
a real black dad,
a really loving black dad,
a black girl dad,
not a perfect guy—
a standup black guy,
an around-the-way black guy,
one who made some money moves to give his black family
 better than he had in his black life.
I come from a black man,
a black dad,
a real black dad,
a really loving black dad,
a black girl dad—
he never served time,
though that would not have canceled his black life value.
Never served time unless you count the military—
dedicated years of his black life to this white, red, and blue
country,

which pretends not to have seen his blackness, or his manness,
dad-ness or his service
he was a retired Air Force master sergeant.
A black man,
a real black dad,
a really loving black dad,
a black girl dad,
a black United States of America service man.
I come from a black man,
a black dad,
a real black dad,
a really loving black dad,
a black girl dad,
and I miss him dearly.
I wonder what he would think about this BLM movement upon us
today.
By the way (BTW): If you take out the "black" from every phrase I
have spoken thus far,
you'll see **that** my dad
my dad who was a *real* man,
my girl-dad is much like yours.)
And I know my dad would be *pained* to see other black men,
real black dads, really loving black dads,
black girl dads,
other round-the-way, inner city, humble-beginning black dads,
like him, still
being persecuted the way they were in black times from his black
youth, and honestly, from his black prime, and sadly, from the
black cusp of his black middle age.
(For that's as far as he got—Life expectancy for men, for black
men,
black male life expectancy is not as lengthy as that of others.
Please stop killing them.
Some judge our kids—

black kids from black single-parent homes, indicating their black
problems come from no **real** black dads in their black homes.
Well—
stop killing them, for just being their black selves, please. I digress.
My dad was a black ***man***;
my dad was a ***black*** man;
my ***dad*** was a black man;
and he mattered—he mattered dearly to me and my black family,
(same as other black dads whose lives were take unjustly by the
untrained, ill-trained, hate trained underbelly (or mainstream) of
this white, red, and blue country. Those black men,
Those real black dads,
Those black girl-dads ***mattered*** if not to you, to somebody
like me, and my black self).
I come from a black man,
a black dad,
 a real black dad,
a black girl-dad, and
I miss him dearly. And Always.
Love always for the black man who spawned me—my real black
dad,
my black girl-dad,
a black, real man. A man's man. A really loving black man,
the first black man to ***love*** me and my black self.
I don't have any black sons.
But this black mom has a black daughter
and I'm privileged to package all the black love
that my black dad gave me
onto and into her, and ***beyond*** her,
as he was a ***really loving black man*** and
he would want this that way.
My black dad enjoyed that purple-bagged Crown on occasion, and,
through my black *child* lens, I remember thinking he looked ***so***
sad in those occasions,

and now, through my black *adult* lens, I have moments when I
wonder what on earth he was reflecting on.
Perhaps it was just the **weight**
of being
a being a black man
a black dad,
a real black dad,
a really loving black dad,
a black girl-dad and perhaps
perhaps he was trying to shed some light on the darkness that other
people's **hate** poured into that. I'm blessed to be able to bestow
onto others all the black lessons and all the black blessins
 that my really, black dad bestowed upon me.
You see,
My daddy was black and he mattered.

Coming Soon: A Short Story
by
I. smith

---

an excerpt from "Where Mountains and Valleys Meet"

"Hope *that* answers your question!" John said to himself, upon beginning his swift walk through her town that he had moved to on their wedding day directly to the post office with an envelope in his hand containing a letter that read:

Dear Pilar:

WHEN I AM READY!

Until next time,
John

Head down as he walked through town, counting audibly and periodically pushing up slipping glasses, with his irate letter to Pilar in hand, John recalled the reason for which he had left the "big city, bright lights," sold his over-priced, high-rise, studio apartment, left the subway, the skyline, the parties, the social life—for her and this no-name town, in which none of his family dwelled. He initially knew only her, Stephanie. She had been his life, his present, his future, his bride. Her family, now his, as his was dead to him. Her lifestyle, her happiness had been of utmost importance to him. His friend had advised him against moving, but love has deaf ears, and Chadwick had not known that Stephanie had been ill. John's recollections of his and Stephanie's courtship were helping to center him along his indignant, peculiar swift walk taken for the purpose of reclaiming his peace, as he could be easily tetchy.

acknowledgments

I would like to acknowledge my loved and trusted family and friends who took the time to read my writing and to provide opinions and support throughout the years. I would like to thank all educators who taught and/or counseled me, starting with my parents—who, though not formal educators, were in fact, my first teachers—my grade schoolteachers, undergrad and grad school professors who directed, challenged, and encouraged me, ultimately giving me desire to continue this author journey. I thank those who published my work and/or who considered publishing it. I thank you, my reader, for finding value in spending time my writing.

www.ingramcontent.com/pod-product-compliance
Lightning Source LLC
Chambersburg PA
CBHW051116300726
48981CB00002B/160